Martha

Karlee Jean-Ann

Published by Karlee Jean-Ann, 2024.

This is a work of fiction. Similarities to real people, places, or events are entirely coincidental.

MARTHA

First edition. May 28, 2024.

Copyright © 2024 Karlee Jean-Ann.

ISBN: 979-8224799763

Written by Karlee Jean-Ann.

I dedicate this book to my wonderful teacher, Mrs. Craft. You once told me your dream was for a student of yours to publish a book. Well, thank you for pursuing your dreams while guiding me to pursue mine.

James

"My first love, my worst mistake."

June 13, 1950

Martha's gaze was set on her husband, James, as she replayed a wonderful scene in her head. The day he proposed. To her it was the most important day of her life, though she doubted James remembered anything of it. The black and white checkered floor, the seats that seemed to squeak every time you sat on them, the sound of burgers sizzling on the grill. She found herself thinking about the past far more than normal. She missed her teens, but her conscience reminded her daily that she could also be longing for James. The James she used to know. The James that would write her silly songs, and make sure to tell her he loved her before shutting his eyes to sleep. The James that cared. She sat on her crimson couch, in her baby pink nightgown that she had yet to change out of. Martha rubbed her sleepless eyes, her thoughts seemed to fade away and all that could be heard now was James, yelling from the kitchen,

"Martha!" anger evident in his voice.

"Yes dear?" A tall, slender man marched into the living room with a brown suit jacket draping from his hand. He was dressed in a white, long sleeve, button up shirt that was tucked into khaki trousers, and a red necktie could be found around his collar. With an outraged expression, he shook the article of clothing in front of Martha's face.

"What is this?!"

Martha's eyes widened, "Oh, well that's George's coat. I suppose he left it here when he came over to help me with the..." Another word didn't dare escape her lips when James began laughing.

"And let me guess, his jacket just fell off didn't it? You didn't think it was important to tell me George would be over, did you? Oh, and you just made sure to have him over *when* I wasn't around, didn't you?" Martha sank back into her spot. James looked as if he was getting closer to her with every word he spoke. "You're a cheat Martha. A good for nothing, cheat." He spat and threw the jacket onto her lap. His brown dress shoes clicked on the floor with each step he took. His head rested in his hand, shaking slightly as he paced the floor. "Do you know who I am Martha?" Too afraid to speak, Martha shook her head in understanding. "I am James Reed, the owner of one of the largest companies in this country. And if word on the street is that James's wife is a little snake, what do you think that's gonna do for my business?" He stared daggers into her, making her feel about the size of an ant.

"I..I didn't cheat on you James. I've known George since I was six, and we've been friends for years." The room was filled with a silence, one of which James felt the need to break. He threw the jacket onto Martha's lap. With his hands stuffed in his pockets and his jaw clenched in anger, he made his way to the door. He yanked his hat from the top of the coat rack with a more than needed force, causing the stand to sway.

"I'll be back later!" he declared, before walking out the door, slamming it behind him. Martha looked at the brown jacket on her lap. Hot tears filled her eyes, a few straying away and leaving a damp trail down her cheek. Soft sobs could be heard throughout the house, though no one was there to listen. She craned her neck to look at the telephone sitting beside her on the coffee table. After the dialing of a few numbers, George's voice could be heard. "Hello?" He croaked, sounding as if he had just awakened from a peaceful sleep. No words passed through Martha's ruby lips, just sniffles and the occasional sob. And though no words were spoken, George knew exactly what was going on. For days, weeks, perhaps even months, George would get phone calls from Martha. Phone calls filled with tears and sobs and sorrow. At first, he wasn't concerned. Women will be women. But as the days grew into weeks, and the stories seemed to be worsening, he had more than slight suspicions. Martha would tell him the stories of how James would come home late, sometimes drunk. How he would mention 'getting back at her' for cheating on him with George, though she did nothing of the sort. As time went on, James's little remarks began implying many things and not so vaguely either. "Other women could treat me better", "I met a lady at the supermarket today, maybe I should be friends with her...like you're friends with George." Over and over, each time his implications became painfully obvious.

"He's seeing someone else, George. I just need evidence." Martha's quavering voice made George's heart ache. Knowing that she was in so much pain because of James made his blood boil.

"I'm sure everything will be fine Martha. He might just be acting odd, maybe he's going through something." George tried to stay positive, show her some kind of hope. But how could he give someone hope when he had none himself?

"I don't know why he woke up mad today. All of the laundry is done, and the dishes are clean." She spoke through a yawn, alternating her words slightly.

"How much sleep did you get last night Martha?" George's voice showed a genuine concern.

"Two, maybe three hours." He could practically hear the shrug of shoulders in her voice.

"Get some sleep Martha." After the exchange of a one-word goodbye, Martha's eyes fluttered shut. Leaving her to lay on the couch, dreaming of that day in the diner, when all things were good.

However, it didn't leave George in the same place. It left him with a mind of curiosity and worry. Thoughts sped through his brain at what seemed to be a million miles a minute. All he could think about the entire day was Martha. He was nagged multiple times by his boss for daydreaming during work. And while he tried to occupy his mind with thoughts of something other than her, it was useless. He spent the day yearning for her voice and her words. He desperately wanted to know what James might say or do the next time. Thankfully, Martha called him once again that night. While four in the morning seemed to be an awfully erratic time to call someone, George was just happy that he was awake to answer.

"He was with her today." As much as it shocked him that she didn't care to say hello, it shocked him more that her voice was steady. Nothing about her tone led George to believe that she was crying or upset this time around.

"Martha, you can't be certain about these things you know." Silence passed some time before she finally answered.

"I know now that I'm not the one he wants. I'm afraid, George. I'm afraid that my thoughts might become reality; I might make my thoughts *become* reality."

"What do you mean Martha?" George completely disregarded the question. Martha decided to end the conversation.

"I'll talk to you tomorrow. I have some...chores to do. Goodbye." Her voice was hesitant as she spoke of the 'chores' she needed to complete.

Though he didn't call back to question her, George was mightily confused. She said that she had done the dishes and the laundry already earlier that day, and what chores could she possibly need to do at four in the morning? But he thought of it no longer. His day had been stressful enough already, and he was ready to climb into his own bed sheets for the night. The night went on peacefully until the sound of someone banging on the door made George sit straight up in his bed. He was breathing heavily and droplets of sweat made his shirt cling to his back. His heart felt like it might jump out of his chest if he didn't calm down. A nightmare. Something that George had experienced quite frequently the past few weeks. He looked at the clock on the wall and noticed it was only seven in the morning. Who might be knocking on the door at seven in the morning? He threw his bed sheets to the side and swung his feet around, so they were dangling off the bed. A red robe with his initials embroidered on it in gold sat to the side on a small wooden chair. He slipped it onto his pale body, as well as his matching red slippers, and trudged to the door. Carefully, he slid the chain to his door lock and peered through a crack in the door. Standing in the cold pouring rain was Martha, frail and shivering slightly.

"Martha? What are you doing here at seven in the morning?" George asked as he allowed the woman to come into his home, away from the cold outdoors.

"Pack your bags," she whispered softly. "mine are already in the car." She nodded towards the window, and in George's driveway sat the car of James Reed.

"Martha what's going on?" She turned to look at George.

"Either you pack your bags, or I'll pack them for you." Her voice was calm, and she smiled sweetly.

"Okay I guess." Though the words were hesitant, George began to pack his bags. George darted his eyes to Martha on the other side of the room. She was fidgeting more than usual, and her gaze didn't dare stray from the window.

"Martha are you okay?" He asked as he carried his suitcases to the door.

"Yes of course. Why wouldn't I be fine? Yes, I'm fine." Her words came out like lightning, George could barely tell what she had said.

"Okay. Now will you tell me why I had to pack my bags?" He asked.

Martha shook her head, "Later George. Right now, we just need to focus on leaving." She opened the door and guided George to walk outside.

"Leave? Where are we going?" He laughed a little, thinking it must simply be a joke.

"How do you feel about Harrisburg, Pennsylvania?" Martha opened the trunk. Inside sat three other suitcases that George assumed to be hers.

"Are you crazy?" He said, outraged. While Harrisburg wasn't an across country trip, they lived in Rhode Island, and Pennsylvania was about six hours away.

"George, never ask me that again. Get in the car and stop asking questions." Martha said as she slid into the driver's seat. George was quiet as they drove the first half hour. His mind was busy trying to connect the dots.

"What is James gonna say about this?" Martha rolled her eyes when she heard the question.

"What did I tell you about asking questions? Besides, we don't have to worry about James." Her grip on the steering wheel tightened and she flashed a forced smile.

"Martha, I need you to talk to me. Did James leave? Did he kick you out?" George was dying to know what was going on.

"Listen George, I'm about to tell you something and if you don't take it to your grave, then I'll be digging your grave for you." Martha had trusted George with all her secrets, and he wondered now what made this one so special. "Okay I promise." George held his hands up as if he was surrendering.

"I killed him." Martha's gaze was on the road the entire time she spoke. George felt his heart drop and his face went pale.

With wide eyes he began to speak, "You what?" He asked, fear in his voice.

"James came home late last night. While he went upstairs and got ready for bed, I was busy doing the laundry. He always wears a white button up shirt to work and as I was putting it in the washing machine, I noticed a stain on the collar. It wasn't a normal stain from food or a pen of some sort, it was a lipstick stain. It wasn't mine either. I hadn't kissed him in months and the lipstick was pink. I wouldn't dare be caught in some flamingo looking pink lipstick. It was an impulse decision George, it really was. Before he went to bed, I slipped just a bit of poison into his nightly glass of milk."

George looked astonished and terrified all at once. "Why did you have poison, Martha?" He asked in a voice close to a whisper.

"We had great trouble with mice in our home. Normal rat poisoning wouldn't work, so I found someone that was willing to sell me real poison. It honestly wasn't that hard." Wasn't hard? It honestly wasn't that hard? George couldn't, wouldn't, believe his ears. Martha had a heart of gold. She wouldn't dare think about the awful act of killing, let alone put it into action.

"Martha, are you sure you killed him?" His voice wasn't steady. How could it be? He was asking Martha, the woman his heart desired to be loved by, if she was a murderer.

The corner of Martha's lips drew upward into a small, wicked smile as she laughed at his question. "Why I'm not sure George. I suppose it takes a doctor to find that a man's heart isn't beating." She spoke with sarcasm dripping from her voice.

"Why are you bringing me with you?" George's heart raced and his hands shook as if he was cold.

"I can't just leave you behind George. What if the police come to you with questions? You'd sit there and tell them that I had issues with James and the case would be closed. I'd probably have wanted posters out all around town. That's why we must move to Pennsylvania." George tried to think about what the next few years of his life would look like. Would he be hiding out in the shadows like he was the killer himself? Or would life in Pennsylvania be the same as it was in Rhode

Island? Would he be able to go to the grocery store without worrying there was a cop there looking for him? It was all too much to handle. He'd just found out his lifelong best friend is now a murderer, and he is running away with her. He tried to rest in the car. Tried to shut his eyes and pretend it was all a dream, but it was impossible.

He awoke from his sleep when the car came to a stop. He rubbed his eyes and yawned, "Where are we?" Martha smiled faintly at the man sitting next to her. He was in such a vulnerable state. Depending on what she said, he would see her as either a murderer or his best friend.

"We're in Pennsylvania. I found a motel room, but I have an apartment lined up for us tomorrow." Martha took George's hand in her own and held it softly. "I know this is all a lot to take in George," she looked at him with stars in her eyes. "but we're going to get through this. Together." Her voice was comforting, yet her words were full of poison. George helped Martha carry their suitcases up the stairs and into their motel room. Inside sat a bed, covered in a yellow polka dot blanket, a nightstand, and a small television. George sat on the edge of the bed and switched on the tv. Martha was sitting on the other side of the room, unpacking her bags and getting ready for bed. The Tv flipped on with a static like sound as it revealed a news reporter sitting in front of his desk.

"Ladies and gentlemen, I have just been informed of heartbreaking news. Mr. James Reed, the owner of the renowned oil company 'Reed Oil Co.' has been reported dead. He was found at 11:08 A.M. at his home in Richmond Rhode Island. The cause of death is undetermined, and police are currently investigating. My heart goes out to his loved ones, he will be missed." George felt his heart drop and he looked over to Martha. A smirk was worn on her face and she giggled like a schoolgirl.

"Martha, you're twenty-five for goodness' sake. You've pretty much ruined your entire life. You think this is funny?" George yelled, not understanding how murder could be amusing to her.

"Yes actually." Martha stood from the floor and walked over to George. "You don't?" George was so mad he thought smoke might blow out his ears. He marched to the door and turned the handle.

"I'm sleeping in the car." he said, voice stern and loud.

"George," Martha called in a sweet voice. "don't think about running to the police. I'll find you." her words were spoken barely above a whisper. It was enough to send a shiver down George's spine. He didn't speak another word, just huffed in anger and slammed the door behind him as he made his way to the car.

David

"They say you can't put a price on love. I suppose I've proved them wrong once again."

May 23, 1953

Martha's soft lips were coated in blood red lipstick as she stared at herself in the vanity. A faint popping sound could be heard as she rubbed her lips together, blending the makeup into her skin.

"I don't understand you Martha. This is the first man you've been romantically involved with for years. And what do you decide to do? Rob him." George hissed.

A chuckle rolled off Martha's tongue. "I'm not in love with him, George. He's in love with me. I don't know about you, but I've learned to take advantage of my opportunities." A smirk appeared upon her face making the corners of her eyes bunch into a wrinkle.

"Listen Martha, we've been through this once and it won't happen again. I won't allow it'. I have dealt with the guilt for far too long. I will not allow you to add more to the mix." George had never been afraid to stand up to Martha until the incident with James a few years prior. Now he followed her around like a puppy that was not yet trained, protected yet one small slip up could cause a ruckus.

Martha's smile suddenly turned to a pout. Her eyes stared at George as though she was now the puppy, looking up at its owner in sadness. "Are you trying to say that I would kill Dave?"

George rolled his eyes, her foolish child-like faces made him sick. "You killed James, Martha. What is supposed to make me believe that you wouldn't do it again?"

"Nothing. Other than the fact that I haven't killed you, and I killed James for a good reason. See George, people like you believe there is no reason to murder. There's no justifiable reason. But George, what was I supposed to do? Let that man who told me for years that I was a good for nothing cheat who couldn't do anything right be with another woman? Behind my back? I'm afraid not George. I took enough criticism from that man every day of my life, and I was not about to let him get away with what he falsely accused me of. If you disagree then you belong six feet under with him." George's heart seemed to skip a beat at those words. Martha would never kill him. Or maybe she would. He had no way of knowing until the day that she showed up with a gun pointed in his direction.

"Martha, I don't agree that what James did was right. I strongly disagree with it...but murdering someone? That's simply not okay. Where did you even meet David?" George was now sitting on the small bed inside of their one room condo.

"I met him at the post office last week when I sent a letter to my mother. We began talking, and I found out that he was a close family friend of ours when I was younger. We exchanged telephone numbers, and he asked me to accompany him to a business gathering tonight. He owns a men's apparel company just down the street from Mel's diner and they're celebrating five years."

George hopped to his feet and shoved his hands into his pockets. "See he sounds like a genuinely nice guy Martha. Why would you ever want to hurt him?" The want to commit a crime was something George would simply never understand, no matter how much Martha tried to explain.

"Who ever said I wanted to hurt him? I know *I* never said anything of the sort. Anyhow, I have a bit of a favor to ask of you, George. I'll write down Dave's address for you, at around eleven thirty you need to be waiting for me in the back alleyway behind his home. Understand?"

George was astonished. Did she really just ask him to be her getaway driver? "Martha, I'm not too sure I want to do this. Just because you have decided to throw your life away being a criminal doesn't mean that I would like to. I'm not going to be your getaway driver."

Martha looked at him with bulging eyes, "I mustn't be hearing correctly, I could have sworn you just told me no." She chuckled a small bit before rising out of her chair. Her midnight black heels made her about two inches taller than George, but at the moment she seemed to tower over him. "You do as I say, not whatever that dumb voice in your head may be telling you. I know what's best for us George, and that's truly all I want, what's best for *us*." Her face was so close to George's that he could pick up the slight scent of her peppermint toothpaste.

"What time did you say to be there?" A defeated look appeared upon George's face, giving him slight frown lines upon his face. It was hard to comprehend the change that had hit Martha's heart those three years ago. What had that man done to give this sweet young girl the mind of a killer? The smile that only she could provide for him had now been stolen and replaced with a dull solemn frown.

"I knew you'd come around to it. It's at eleven thirty, be there by eleven just in case." Martha kissed his cheek as a form of gratitude, leaving a small red mark in the shape of her lips. She looked at a clock on the wall beside her, "I should really get going, I'll see you there."

Just like that Martha was out the door, heading off to commit yet another crime for which she felt no sorrow.

●●●

Extravagant things were never something Martha was used to. She grew up in a home where the next meal wasn't guaranteed. Her mother worked hard in a factory, slaving away to make the money her father would spend at a casino instead of his children's meals and medical care. Her house was barely a proper living facility. Every bucket and bowl to her family's name was occupied by a dripping hole in the roof. She slept on the floor, a thin fleece blanket being the only thing to keep her warm in the cold winter months. Christmas was never something she was excited for. All of the children at school showed off their new toys they had received while all she had to show were her beaten up rags of an outfit. She held shame in her family's misfortune and always swore she would have nicer things in her adult life.

As Martha stepped into the home of David Whitmer she was hit with an overwhelming feeling of awe. The house was practically a mansion. Large scale angel paintings covered the tall ceiling, dark green velvet drapes hung on the windows, near black wood lined the walls and floor leading the way to a spiral staircase in the corner of the room, Martha had never witnessed something so beautiful in her life.

Her black tulle dress draped across the floor as she walked, caressing the wooden planks slightly with each step she took. A dress this elegant would have never been in her budget, but she decided that the money she was about to endure would be worth it. As she made her way to the dining room, she examined all the people around. Most of them were mingling, holding a drink in one hand and using the other to express the words coming out of their mouth. She stood on the side of the room, taking in the scent of whiskey and cigarettes.

"Martha?" a deep voice called her name from behind her. She turned to see David standing there with a smile and an open hand.

She put her hand in his and watched as he brought it to his lips and kissed it softly before allowing it to fall at her side once again.

"I thought about looking for you, but I figured you'd catch up to me eventually." She said, a smirk on her face.

"Well it looks like I've found you then, haven't I?" Dave lifted his brow ever so slightly as he asked his question, his playful tone of voice adding to the conversation. He held out his arm, subtly suggesting that Martha would walk with him. She wrapped her arm around his and followed him back into the living room toward the staircase.

"I've never been in such a nice home, David. It must have cost you a fortune." Martha stared at him with her piercing hazel eyes.

"Well I suppose it did cost me a pretty penny. Personally, I think it was worth every cent. I'd love you to show you around, if you'd like me to of course."

Martha smiled sweetly at his kindness, "I'd love to."

Dave led Martha up the spiral staircase, holding her hand behind him all the way up. They passed a few paintings along the way portraying scenes of angels and different colored flowers spread across a table or sitting in a vase, some of the prettiest artwork to grace Martha's eyes.

Martha followed David down multiple narrow hallways, listening contently as he blabbered of the history behind each and every room.

"This, right here, is my office. It's where I do all of my work and keep all of my valuables, if you know what I mean. It's not really an important room; the only valuables I have are some extra cash and a necklace from my mother."

Martha was instantly intrigued. She had listened to this man go on about the fascinating history of this house for close to an hour now, and she was beginning to get annoyed.

"Your mother left you a necklace?" A questioning tone to her voice.

"Yes actually, before she passed. Though it has monetary value, the sentimental value means the most to me. The necklace would go for close to a hundred dollars for anyone looking for the specific stone, but I would never sell it. It means too much to me." He smiled softly at the memory of his mother wearing her favorite necklace before she passed away.

"Would you mind if I looked at it? I understand it must be a very valuable thing to you. I obviously would respect your decision whatever that may be, but I'd love to see it sometime. I bet it's beautiful!"

David studied Martha for a moment, seemingly evaluating the woman in his head.

"I suppose that would be alright. Mother would have wanted me to share the beauty with someone other than myself."

Martha watched carefully as he pulled a small box from his desk, something that looked close to a suitcase. He slowly turned the knob at the front of the box. Right, left, right, right. Four digits. Martha quietly shut the door behind her, careful not to cause a lack of concentration for the man.

Martha's heels tapped against the cold wooden floor as she came to stand behind David. She placed her hand on his shoulder softly, showing him that she was there. The box clicked open slightly before being opened completely and revealing the diamond necklace within the case. It was beautiful, small gleams of light bounced from the stones and reflected making them shine brighter than stars. Beside the necklace, lay three blank white envelopes Martha assumed to hold the "extra cash" Dave had spoken of beforehand. After taking a moment to bask in the beauty of the diamonds, Martha finally set her plan into action. In one swift motion she quickly grabbed a hardcover book off of David's desk and hit him in the head. He fell to the ground with a loud thump and touched his head. A small stream of blood came from just above his eyebrow.

His voice quivered with fear, "Martha what are you doing?" His eyes searched the woman's face for a reason as to why she was behaving this way.

Martha didn't say a word. She stepped towards David, a sinister smile on her face. Slowly and carefully she reached for the small wooden desk chair positioned next to her. Using all her strength she hurled the chair towards

David. He tried to protect himself by raising his arms, but it was no use. It hit him directly in the head, giving him a bloody nose and a shaken-up expression.

"Martha, think about what you're doing, please!" he yelled.

Martha crouched next to him on the floor, placing her hand over the man's mouth and nose.

"I really didn't want to have to do this David. I think you're a great man, and I can promise you now your mother's necklace will be in good hands,." she smiled sweetly at him.

Dave struggled to stand, but he was slowly going unconscious.

"Stop fighting Dave. It's okay." Martha whispered, her devilish voice filling the air.

She watched as David's eyes closed, his chest sitting still. Martha giggled evilly before standing up and heading to the desk. She scoffed as she looked down on the blood that was on her hand.

"Why did your nose have to bleed?" she asked looking at David's cold body, "I was hoping there would be no blood."

Marth snatched the safe off the wooden desk, but before heading to the door she took one closer look at David. She tilted her head slightly, examining him as if wondering what she might do next. Slowly, she leaned down and kissed David's forehead, leaving her scarlet red signature on his skin. She then headed to the door and made her way downstairs making sure not to draw attention to herself.

As she reached the end of the spiral staircase, she glanced at a clock placed on the wall, eleven twenty-eight, just on time. Her heels snapped harshly against the floor as she made her way to the back door leading to the alleyway.

Sitting in the gray rubble of the alleyway was George, waiting in the driver's seat of his dim black Jaguar XK 150. Martha quickly jumped into the passenger's seat in time to realize police had arrived outside of the home.

"George drive, now." Martha's voice was stern, and her eyes had a tinge of panic.

George stepped on the gas making the car jolt forward suddenly. "What's that?" George asked, pointing to the small box resting in Martha's lap.

"His valuables." she replied, not bothering to look at George.

Martha turned in her seat to see a cop car following close behind.

"Martha what is going on? Why are they chasing us?" George practically yelled, staring at Martha with fear in his eyes.

"Someone must have found him and called the cops." she whispered, mostly to herself.

"What do you mean they must've found him? You said you were robbing him, what is there to find?"

Martha failed to respond to his questions, she simply stared into the distance of the road and trees ahead.

George waved his hand in front of Martha's face, "Martha you need to tell me what is going on right now." The car bounced and sloshed side to side as George turned onto a dirt road, pushing the gas pedal as hard as possible. The police that had been chasing them were sure to come around the corner eventually, but for now they had bought themselves some time.

"I did a little more than rob him," Martha confessed, holding out her bloody hand. "I really didn't intend to kill him."

George slammed on the brake pedal causing Martha's knees to jam into the dash.

George gripped the steering wheel so hard his knuckles turned white, "Get out."

"Excuse me?" Martha looked at him puzzled.

"I said get out Martha. I told you I wasn't going to do this again and I meant it. I am not about to be part of your little scheme. I don't know where the happy girl I used to know went, but you need to bring her back. Now get out of my car."

Martha was astonished. After all they had been through together, he was really going to try and get rid of her? "Oh George," she chuckled. "I don't know who you take me for, but I am not leaving. I've killed two grown men that were twice my size and frankly George, you're the same size as me if not smaller. If you think you have authority over me you need to check again, now get to driving."

George grit his teeth, "Where to?" He couldn't believe he was actually about to listen to this woman. What had he become? A slave to her commands? Nonetheless, he waited for an answer.

"Fort Wayne, Indiana."

Robert

*"If there is one thing my father did teach me, it was to never trust
a stranger."*

November 13, 1954

The harsh cold air hit Martha's cheek, turning her face bright crimson. She tried not to slip on ice as she carried a small woven basket full of clothes across the street to Bennet's Laundromat. Since Martha left Rhode Island she hadn't performed any womanly activities such as laundry, cleaning up around the house, or even cooking decent meals. Her diet now consisted of frozen foods and TV dinners that took merely any time in the oven. Though it was nice to take a break, she felt George deserved at least a little bit of appreciation for dealing with her. That's why today she decided to take the clothes to get cleaned and make George a home cooked meal. As she opened the laundromat door a small gold bell chimed above her. The building smelled of tide laundry detergent and cigarettes, considering mostly everyone there was smoking one. Martha's black heels thudded against the detergent stained tile flooring as she lugged the basket towards a vacant washer. Nevertheless, she carried on with what she came for.

She smiled at a man next to her while she began to put her clothing into the machine. A colorful sign on the wall read "Two loads for only 25¢!"

Martha searched her coat pockets for a quarter but began to get very frustrated when she wound up empty handed.

"Do you need a quarter miss?" A squeaky voice called.

Martha looked over to see a small, thin man with fiery orange hair sitting on a bench staring at her through his metal rimmed glasses.

"Pardon?" she said, wondering if he was talking to her.

"I asked if you needed a quarter. I saw that you didn't have one in your pockets and thought I might as well offer." He presented a kind smile.

"Staring at me, were you?" Martha questioned playfully.

The man's face flushed bright red from embarrassment. "Well no, I was just... uhm I wasn't meaning to stare just..."

He was cut off by Martha's airy laugh, "It's okay I understand. I would very much appreciate a quarter if you have one to spare."

The man reached out his arm and placed a quarter in Martha's hand. "I'm Robert by the way," he said shyly.

Martha nodded at him slightly, "Nice to meet you Robert. I'm Martha. Not that it's any of my business, but shouldn't your wife be here doing this for you?"

Robert chuckled to himself, "I don't have a wife."

Martha smiled to herself, a new opportunity. "Oh, you don't? What's a handsome man like you doing out here alone?"

Robert seemed to be the bashful type, blushing intensely at the compliment he had just received. "Well thank you, I'm afraid not many women think that way. How about you? Are those your husband's clothes?" He pointed to George's clothes spinning in the washing machine.

"Oh no, he's just my friend. We've known each other since we were little, and we've been living with each other for a while now to save on expenses." Though this was partially true,

Martha knew she really only kept George around to help her get away from the problems she had created for herself.

"Well goodness I'd think a pretty lady like you would have to have a husband. You've never been married?" He asked.

This was where it got tricky. Though some people felt bad for her 'loss' of James, others found it very unattractive that she had been married before. "My husband sadly passed away about four years ago, I miss him more every day." A sorrowful look graced her face.

"I'm so sorry for your loss, Martha. I'm sure he was a great man." Robert's eyebrows furrowed as he spoke.

"Thank you very much. I try not to speak of the incident, it was very traumatic for me." Martha's voice quivered as a single tear streamed down her cheek.

Martha Lynn Clark was not only magnificent at lying, but also acting. During grade school she participated in all the plays, musicals, and other theatrical events that she could, and over time she became very good. Making herself cry on command was one of her specialties. She was an utterly excellent con artist.

"Oh Martha, don't cry. Here, take a seat." Robert patted the spot next to him on the bench, welcoming her to a seat.

Martha ushered herself over to the bench and sat down. Robert pulled a small gray handkerchief from the back pocket of his trousers and handed it to Martha.

"Thank you. I'm sorry. I really shouldn't even be sharing this with you, I mean we don't even know each other." She sniffled quietly.

"No, no, it's okay honestly. I want to help whenever I can." He flashed a warm smile.

Martha looked beyond the man at a stack of papers that were marked with pencil.

"What's that?" she asked, pointing to the papers.

"Oh these?" Robert picked up the papers and handed them to Martha. "It's just a book I'm editing at the moment. I'm a copyeditor for a publishing company in Indianapolis."

Bingo! "So, you help people get their books published?" Martha's tears had vanished, and she now seemed more excited than ever.

"In a way, yes, I suppose you could say that." He stared at Martha intensely. What could she ever want with a book publisher?

"Well I've been working on a book myself. I'm an aspiring writer and my dream is to get a book of my own on the shelves. Do you think you could take a look at it for me and maybe see about getting it published?" She spoke as if she were a giddy child.

"That shouldn't be a problem. I don't have many books to edit at the moment, one more couldn't hurt." Robert's blue eyes were glowing with excitement. No one, especially not beautiful women, seemed interested in his career.

"Thank you so much! I'm ecstatic. My house is just across the street, I can get you a copy of the book and we'll be back before our clothes are done in the dryer. Is that alright?"

Robert's better judgment told him that he had only known this woman a short amount of time and following her to her home was probably not the best idea, but he felt bad turning her down. "I suppose that would be alright." He said, a nervous smile upon his face.

"Wonderful." Martha stood and handed the papers back to Robert before heading for the door.

Robert followed after her hesitantly. He rushed in front of Martha in order to open the door for her.

"A gentleman huh?" Martha giggled.

As they approached the slick icy road Martha snatched Robert's hand and ran across the street with him. Robert was taken by surprise, but he wasn't exactly upset about holding her hand.

Robert looked up to see a small, pale yellow house. White shutters with small diamond details framed the windows and the branches of what he assumed to be shrubs lined the front lawn.

Martha's keys jangled in her hand as she struggled to unlock the front door and open it, guiding Robert inside. George was currently at work, and he wouldn't be home for a while. So, there was no need to worry about him popping in randomly.

"This is a wonderful little home you have here," Robert commented as he admired the brick fireplace.

Two burnt red loveseats faced each other in front of the fireplace, a small light wood coffee table was placed between them.

"Please take a seat." Martha said as she walked towards a small pinewood bookshelf that sat in the corner of the room.

Robert sat down on a loveseat and warmed up by the fire as he waited for Martha.

"So, what kind of book have you written?" He questioned.

"Oh, I am so irresponsible. I would lose my head if it weren't attached to my neck. I'm afraid I left it in George's briefcase. He's the friend I told you about, who lives here with me. Well since you're here you might as well stay a moment to get warm. I have a different book that was written by my grandfather, would you like to take a look at it?" Martha raised her brow.

"Oh, that's alright I really should get going anyhow." Robert tried to stand but Martha quickly cut him short.

"No," Her voice suddenly became stern and forceful. "I mean why don't you just have a cup of coffee with me and check it out? My grandfather would have really appreciated it if he were still here. He always said he never felt his book got enough recognition." She tilted her head to the side and smiled sweetly at him.

Robert now felt guilty saying no, "I really can't stay long. But I suppose if it meant a lot to your grandfather, I could look it over."

Martha smiled wickedly to herself and grabbed a random book from the shelf, *When My Soul Will Rest* by Jonathan Rigby. Martha handed Robert the book and headed into the kitchen.

"Jonathan Rigby? You're part of the Rigby family? I've read a few books by your grandfather then. He's a wonderful author, truly one of my favorites." Robert turned the book over and began reading the description, interested in what it might be about.

"Would you like some coffee Rob? Is it alright if I call you that?" Martha called from the kitchen.

"I'd love some. And yes, you can call me whatever you'd like." He smiled to himself slightly.

MARTHA

Martha opened her silverware drawer and ran her hand over her collection of cooking knives. Multiple knives with different blades; serrated, sharp, dull, long, short, jagged, smooth. Eventually her fingertips landed upon a large chef's knife with a dark wood handle.

"Would you like cream in your coffee?" Martha asked as she pulled the knife from the drawer and held it behind her back.

"That would be nice, thank you." Robert was still busy in the living room, reading the first chapter of his book.

Martha carried a small white coffee cup into the room carefully with her one hand. She stood behind the loveseat where Robert was enjoying his book, watching over his shoulder as he licked his finger and turned the page.

"Here's your coffee." She said quietly, careful not to break his concentration.

"Oh, thank you." Robert whispered, too invested in his book to care about his surroundings or anything going on around him.

Slowly, Martha took the knife from behind her and hovered it behind Robert's back. A loud gasp echoed against the living room walls as a sharp piercing pain struck through Robert's back and chest.

Martha's lips brushed against Robert's ear, "You should really learn to never trust strangers. Didn't your mother teach you not to follow random people to their homes?" A viscous laugh rolled off Martha's tongue.

As Martha pulled the knife from his back Robert's body slumped over. There he lay, lifeless with a shocked expression cemented upon his face.

• • •

Martha adjusted her rearview mirror, smiling to herself when she saw Robert's body slumped across the back seat.

"It really is a shame, you know. All of the people who sent their book to you in hopes of becoming famous authors will have to wait a while longer. I almost feel sorry for them. I'm glad you didn't have a wife and children though. I would never be able to kill someone's father." Martha spoke calmly, watching the trees pass by her window as she drove deeper into the woods.

"Oh, and just so you know I'm not part of the Rigby family. I'm part of the Clark family. Quite honestly, I have no idea who the Rigby's are, but I'm sure they would have done a better job raising me than my no-good father. He never cared much about my siblings or me. He was more concerned with alcohol and gambling. Anywho now that you've gotten to know me for who I really am, why don't you tell me about yourself?" Martha smiled contently awaiting a response from Robert, though he was obviously incapable of responding.

"Cat got your tongue?" She cackled to herself. "Well, it looks like we're here Rob." Martha put the car into park and hopped out of the driver's seat. She popped the trunk and grabbed a flat shovel.

"You better cooperate with me," she huffed as she opened the backseat door and began dragging Robert's body into the woods.

• • •

Martha sat George's plate of spaghetti and meatballs down on the table next to his napkin, silverware, and glass of milk. George never complained about TV dinners or the house being dirty, but Martha knew it bothered him. For the past few years, he had occasionally tried to make home cooked food himself, nearly burning the house down with each attempt.

Martha could tell George had missed the way his life used to be and out of the kindness of her heart, she wanted to try and bring it back for him for a small while. Just as she sat her own plate onto the table, George arrived home.

"I'm home." His tired voice called. Though the workday had burned him out and left him longing for his bed, the smell of a home cooked meal always caught his attention.

"Take a seat George." Martha smiled at him and pulled out his seat.

"Well what's all this?" He asked with surprise and excitement evident in his voice.

"I figured you might enjoy a nice meal every now and then, I know you never really get them anymore." Martha anxiously laughed and sat at her seat, sipping her glass of water slowly.

George sat down and began to eat. Martha had really surprised him this time. She was never rude or mean to him, but she never showed him the kindness she had all those years ago. Right now, he saw a bit of the old girl he used to love, and it made him happier than ever.

"How was work?" Martha asked, trying to stray away from the obvious details she might have to tell him soon.

"Exhausting. We didn't have one of the items I needed to fix a woman's sink and she had a complete meltdown, telling me it was my fault and that she would be contacting the company's owner." Plumbing wasn't a job George enjoyed, no plumber truly did, but in times like these it was the best he could do to keep himself off the streets.

"How about you? Seems like you had a pretty busy day yourself." He waved around the clean house.

"Oh, it was alright. Nothing much happened." Martha moved her food around her plate with her fork, as if moving a meatball from one side to the other would make it vanish instantly.

"Come on Martha, tell me something. You always tell me about your day and they're usually much less eventful than today." George smiled at her kindly, trying to pry something out of her.

"Well, I did the laundry at the laundromat across the street. I met a nice man there; his name was Robert." She smiled like a middle school girl with her first boyfriend.

Immediately George's heart dropped. The past two times Martha had ever talked about men with him was when she had killed them.

"That's nice. Did you two exchange contacts?" Somewhere in George's heart he still hoped Martha would find the right man and settle down, though her past relationships hadn't gone as planned.

"No, sadly. We didn't get the chance to. He did come over for a while though, we talked over a cup of coffee." Martha's eyes darted across the room, looking for something, anything, to focus on other than George.

"Will you continue to talk and see each other?" George stuffed another forkful of food into his mouth.

"No, I'm afraid not. He had a little incident, and we won't be seeing each other again."

That was it. That was all George needed to hear to know what was coming next.

"What did you do Martha? Actually, I don't even want to know how you did it, where did you put him? His body?" George's jaw clenched and his hand balled into a fist on the table.

Martha didn't answer, she simply looked at him and smiled. George looked around him, hoping to find an answer as to where she could have hidden the body. As he looked down at his plate and saw his half-eaten meatball he felt his stomach churn, and he thought he might be sick.

"Martha did you..." He didn't dare finish his sentence, he simply pointed to the remaining food on his plate.

"George, I know that I have committed some awful crimes, but I would never and I mean *never* partake in the awful act of cannibalism. I buried him in the woods just north of here." She stood and took the dishes to the kitchen, not giving George enough time to respond.

George stood to his feet, pushing his chair back and paraded into the kitchen. "What do you think you're doing?" George yelled. "Martha you are twenty-nine for goodness sake, and you have already thrown your life away! Where are we supposed to go now? Where?" He was screaming so loud his words became mutilated.

"George, I am a twenty-nine-year-old woman. I know what I am doing. My father threw his life away, I am *not* my father. Besides, I've always wanted to visit Green Bay, Wisconsin."

Paul

"Who knew stains were so hard to get rid of."

July 5, 1956

The warm orange sun peeked its way through the cream-colored blinds, gracing Martha's cheek as she lay in bed. Her pale blue eyes fluttered open and she watched as the fly on her wall inspected every tiny blue flower printed into the wallpaper. Ever since George and Martha made it to Wisconsin, they've been on the lookout for a house. When George quit his job in Indiana, he had no new occupation sitting around waiting for him. Any jobs were hard to come by, especially when you had a record of quitting past ones abruptly. Once Martha saw a small one-bedroom apartment with a kitchen attachment for rent, she pounced on it. And thanks to David's safe, George and Martha had enough money to last a couple weeks while George was looking for a job. Eventually, George got a job as a mechanic a few blocks away from the apartment.

Martha stretched her freckled arms out into the room, yawning as she did so. Her shoulder length brunette hair was tangled and frizzy from her pillow the night before. As she sat up in bed her stomach grumbled, and she checked the clock. One thirty-seven P.M. Usually by now she would have gotten dressed, made the bed, and eaten breakfast and lunch. Lunch. Martha swung her feet over the side of the bed, feeling the plush blue carpet snake between her toes as she stood up.

Rubbing her eyes, she walked to her small oak wood dresser that she shared with George. She slid the top drawer open and began looking through her assortment of clothing. A teal pair of shorts caught her eye and she pulled them from the dresser. Draping the shorts over her arm, she continued to look for a shirt. A cherry red button up blouse with a triangle collar sat neatly folded at the bottom of the drawer collecting dust.

She pulled the shirt from the drawer and rested her outfit upon the baby blue comforter on her bed. Martha slipped out of her nightgown, leaving it to lay on the floor, and began to dress herself for the day.

Ever since the move, Martha hadn't been able to do much. She lay in bed all day, admiring every little flower on the walls of her bedroom like the fly she'd seen that morning. And while Martha said she was simply feeling ill, George insisted otherwise.

He had said that, "The illness was from guilt," and "the murders are catching up to her."

But Martha refused. If she truly felt remorse for the tragedies she had caused, wouldn't she know so? Wouldn't she turn herself in to the authorities and apologize on live television for the murders of all those men? Most certainly she would, and that was why Martha knew that whatever it was she was feeling, it wasn't guilt.

The polished red button of Martha's blouse slid into place with the fabric, closing Martha's shirt completely. Martha looked at herself in the mirror, tucking her shirt into her shorts and straightening it as she did so. She leaned down, rolling the bottoms of her shorts and making them hit at about three inches above her knee.

Her stomach whined again, reminding her that she needed to eat something. Though Martha had never been to Wisconsin until now, and she barely knew her way around, she remembered a sign she saw on the way here from Indiana. The Golden Spoon Diner. It was merely a ten-minute walk from her house, and she needed the sunshine after being cooped up in bed for so long.

Martha laced up her black and white saddle shoes and headed out the door. The Wisconsin sun was one that she hadn't seen before, though she knew it shone the same in all parts of the Earth, she loved seeing it from a different point of view.

As she waltzed along the sidewalk, she made sure not to step on a single crack, counting how many steps she could take inside a single square before she had to step into a new one. The answer was two; she could take two steps.

From any other person's point of view Martha was a cheerful, almost childlike person. She had a good personality and a charm about her that made you want to be in her presence, and that's what she loved so much about herself. She loved that people felt as if they could trust her, and she took advantage of it.

Martha looked up to see a long rectangular building with a glistening golden spoon placed on top. She opened the heavy glass door and could instantly smell the aroma of food inside calling her name.

"Welcome to The Golden Spoon!" An eager, enthusiastic voice called from behind the diner counter.

Martha stood at the door, rocking back and forth from her heels to her toes, watching as the leather of her shoes creased when she leaned forward. She looked up to see a tall man with shaggy brunette hair stumbling towards her in a hurry.

"I'm Paul, I'll be your server today." He flashed a crooked smile and extended his arm to Martha, a shiny grease stained menu in hand.

Martha smirked at the incompetent man and withdrew the menu from his reach.

"Follow me this way, miss." Paul stepped in front of Martha, motioning her to follow him with his arm. As he approached a ruby red leather booth, Paul snatched the pad of paper from the apron tied around his waist. "What can I get for you on this fine evening?" He smiled widely, showing all of his off-white, crooked teeth.

"You mean other than your telephone number?" Martha shone a sly smile and raised her brow as she looked up at the man before her.

Paul chuckled, "Well, ma'am, sadly my boss informed me last week that I'm not allowed to share that information with customers due to that being personal information." He slipped a folded-up napkin onto the table as his eyes darted around the room, looking for whom Martha assumed to be his boss.

Martha giggled and slipped the napkin into her shorts pocket as she too looked around for the man whom she couldn't put a face to yet.

"Now, what would you like to eat?" Paul stood at the corner of the table; arm perched with his pen in hand, ready to write down her order.

"I think I'll have a chocolate milkshake please," Martha sat the menu onto the table instead of into Paul's hand. She hated touching the grease that had built up on the pages.

"Not very hungry, huh? Well, that's alright! I think a shake sounds wonderful." Paul took hold of the menu, showing no care in the world about the grease that now invaded his hands. "That'll be out shortly," he smiled warmly and marched away towards the kitchen.

Martha sighed and rested her head upon her hand. Though she had felt hunger as she entered the diner, a completely new feeling of affection washed over her. Though she never believed in love at first sight, Martha did, however, believe that if it was real, she just witnessed it.

Though she barely knew anything about Paul or who he was, she loved everything about him. He seemed kind and though he wasn't very articulate, he had a personality that drew her to him though she'd known him for merely ten minutes.

Martha's stomach flooded and bloomed with a feeling she had never felt before. Butterflies. She knew this because she had heard her mother talk about it when she was a young girl.

She'd always say, "One day you'll find a man who'll give you butterflies. *Those* are the good ones."

"Here you go, Miss." Paul sat a large glass with an orange swirly straw in front of Martha and shoved his hands deep into his pants pockets. "Anything else I can do for you?" His voice was light and airy, and it had a certain ring to it that was sweet like honey to Martha's ears.

"What time do you get off your shift?" Martha didn't know the words would come out of her mouth, though Paul didn't seem to mind.

"Around two thirty, why?" He smiled at Martha, as if it was a funny question to ask. Considering this chance encounter between the two individuals, Martha knew it was. "I really like your personality. I'd love it if we could get to know each other more. Maybe you could come back to my place? We could, uhm, hang out... if you know what I mean?" Martha batted her big innocent eyes at Paul, hoping anything could save her from the embarrassment she would endure if she got turned down by a fast-food employee.

Paul looked at his feet as if to question his own judgment before answering with a short and simple, "Alright. Just write down your address so I can meet ya' there." He grinned ear to ear and waited patiently for Martha to scribble her address onto an already stained napkin.

Martha copied Paul's previous motion and slid the napkin over to him on the table. "I'll be looking forward to seeing you." She shone a radiant smile and watched as he walked away.

Back at home, *or what little she had of a home,* Martha swept the cracked tile kitchen floor. *Blue Suede Shoes* from Elvis' studio album spun on the record player behind her, and her hips swayed to the music as the bristles of the broom danced across the floor.

There was a knock on the door, and she stood up, leaving the broom leaning on the tabletop in the kitchen. "Coming!" She hollered and straightened out her blouse with her already clammy hands.

Martha blew out a deep breath and opened the creaky old door. Her face flushed at the sight of him, still dressed in his work apron and jeans, still carrying the crooked smile he had at the diner.

"You know what I was thinking on the way over here? I never even caught your name." Paul chuckled a bit and allowed himself into the small kitchen where he took a seat at a teal bar stool.

"Oh," Martha laughed and breathed heavily while she closed the door. Nerves had never hit her this hard. She could have a man at her complete mercy, begging for her to make the 'right' decision and feel nothing at all. Not nerves nor anxiousness, nor sadness. "Well, I'm Martha. I know you're probably thinking about how small the house is, I'm afraid that you've caught me in one of my low times." Martha turned around and examined Paul with her eyes.

Paul didn't seem to be the brightest person. But in all reality, most people probably wouldn't view her as the smartest either. One thing she did like about Paul is that he didn't seem to be bothered by how small her so-called house was. He didn't mind that the carpet was turning up in the corners or that the wallpaper was faded and peeling, he was just glad to be there.

"Oh no! Actually, I was just thinking about where you sit since you ain't got a couch." He chuckled and pointed around the room until his eyes met an old white door, blotted and tattered by smoke from years past. "Is that your living room?" Paul stood from his bar stool and made his way over to the door, not caring to ask Martha if it would be okay.

"No, Paul, that's my bedroom and I would appreciate it if you didn't go in there at the moment, please." Martha followed after Paul, catching up with him only to find he had already opened the door.

"This is a nice little room you have here; I like the blue flowers on the wallpaper." He smiled charmingly while he scanned the room.

"Well, I appreciate the compliments, but I think it's time for you to leave the bedroom please." Martha shoved her hands into her back pockets and stood by the doorway, waiting for Paul to go back into the kitchen.

"Well hey what's this little thing?" Paul's eyes everted to a small, black leather notebook sitting on the bedside table. Next to it sat a bulky black and gold pen.

"I told you not to come in here, Paul." Martha suddenly felt a glint of worry spark in her mind. Her hands clammed up and she wiped them on her shorts, trying to push away the fact that she, Martha Clark, endured the feeling of anxiousness.

Paul reached for the notebook and held it in his hand, examining the texture of the leather under his fingertips. He slipped the cover open and turned the first page. "You keep a diary or somethin'? I thought they were just for little girls." He shrugged his shoulders and began reading the first page.

James,

My first love, my worst mistake. Something about him got under my skin. From the day we met I had always wanted more than what I had. He reminded me of my father in ways, which made my blood boil to just be in the same room as him.

"Nobody is supposed to read that Paul. Hand me it now." Martha reached for the book, but Paul begrudgingly held it in his grip. He turned his back to her and continued reading, blocking her entirely.

Once I found out he truly was seeing another woman I was conflicted with what to do next. My heart told me to

leave him and never turn back. Leave him sitting in the dust so to say, but my brain strongly disagreed. All in all, I still loved James. He was the only family I really had other than my mother, but of course she didn't bother calling often.

"Give me it now Paul!" Martha shrieked as she reached around the man multiple times, fighting to take back the book that contained all of her untold secrets. Paul shoved her with his elbow slightly, causing Martha to stumble backwards and bump into the wall behind her.

"It's just a book Martha; it isn't a big deal." Paul gave her a look of pity as if he was sorry for the stupidity Martha contained to be worrying over this book. He continued to read,

I knew that getting back at him with another man wouldn't work since I, one, didn't know of any men that would agree to such a thing and two, didn't want to deal with the consequences James would give me. I ultimately decided that if I wasn't good enough for James Reed then no one would be. I placed a small amount of poison into his milk before he slept and without any cries for help or blood to clean, he was done for.

Paul's face turned pale white. He turned around to see Martha standing in the doorway with a shiny silver pistol pointed directly at him. She stepped towards him, not faltering her hold on the gun's handle.

"I didn't want to do this Paul, but you just don't know how to listen. I really liked you, Paul. I did. You were going to be my changing point. The point where I could put this all behind me and live my life like a normal woman. But you had to screw it up. You know too much now Paul. Give me the book. Now!"

Paul slipped the book into Martha's free hand and lifted his hands into the air. "It's not too late Martha. You can be a normal woman. We can put this behind us.

You must let me help." Paul stepped forward slowly, careful not to startle Martha into pulling the trigger.

"Don't move Paul." Martha spoke through gritted teeth, not wanting to say more than she needed to about the matter.

Paul scooted his foot forward on the dull carpet, trying to get close enough that he could take the gun from her grasp.

The loud pop of a gun could be heard, and Paul's body fell to the floor. Blood began to pool around his body, staining the carpet a wickedly dark red.

Martha stood at the foot of Paul's body, still holding the gun with shaky hands. She dropped the gun on the bed and closed the door behind her, turning the lock of the door handle.

"Why did I use a gun?" Martha whispered, "Almost anything is easier to clean than a blood wound." Martha searched the bedroom for anything that could help her clean. She quickly flung open the drawer on her bedside table and pulled out a small, dull white rag. On her hands and knees, she began to scrub the floor. She watched as the once white cloth turned a sickly deep red.

"Come out, come out." Martha whispered concerningly.

The front door slammed, and George's voice echoed through the small kitchen, "Martha?" He yelled.

Martha could hear George's loud footsteps against the tile of the kitchen. They got louder, closer, until she could sense him outside of her door. The door handle jostled, and George knocked on the stained wooden surface,

"Martha what's going on? Are you okay?"

"Uhm, I'm fine George." Martha's voice quivered and she stood there still, not daring to move an inch.

"Open the door, Martha." George pounded loudly on the door, making it shake.

"Just wait a while please, I'll be out in a minute!" Martha yelled.

The door burst open with a loud crash and George tumbled to the floor. He had broken it. It couldn't have been too hard, Martha thought, since the door was old and frail.

George's eyes averted to Paul's limp body, laying in the pool of blood on the floor as it had before. He then glanced at the gun laying on the bed. George turned around, made a circle around the kitchen, and walked back into the bedroom.

"Damn it, Martha!" He bellowed, his face was red, and veins seemed to pop out of his neck. "I won't do this anymore!" He lifted his arm up and shook a fist at Martha.

"I had to, George. He wouldn't leave the house." She pleaded with George, wishing his anger might go away.

George sat on the bed and rested his jaw in his hands. He shook his head and stared at the wall, "You're going to get caught one of these days you know." He didn't intend it as a question, just a simple statement that had to be said.

"And why might that be?" Martha leaned her back against the wall, crossing her arms and listening intently. "I won't get caught, George, not unless you slip up. Which you won't do. Will you, George?" She cocked her head slightly to the side and fixed her eyes on George.

There it was. There was the part of Martha that didn't care who or what you were, she was heartless towards you and only cared about herself.

"Don't try to pull that stunt on me Martha. I know you too well. Listen, I'm not going to turn you in. Though you give me every reason not to, somewhere I still find love for you in my heart. I'm just telling you for your own good. Have you ever heard of John Christie?"

"I don't believe so. Why?" Martha rolled her eyes slightly, simply not caring about the conversation.

"He killed over eight people within the span of ten years. But guess what happened to him, Martha?" George stood now, feeling more confident in the point he knew he could make.

"Hm?" Martha hummed.

"He was caught and executed. Killed. Done for. He was hanged. I bet the idea of getting found never even occurred to him. Never crossed his mind. Much like you Martha. You sit here and kill these men that you don't even know. Think about their families. Their mothers, their fathers. You don't know them Martha, but yet you sit here and take their life like it makes yours better. I will never understand why you do what you do, all I know is that someday it will catch up with you and you will be the one with a noose around your neck." A speckle of saliva hit Martha's cheek and George walked out of the room.

She watched in silence as he grabbed his coat from the counter, slipped on his shoes, and walked out the door.

Henry

"Until death do us part is a silly saying."

October 27, 1957

George's hand slammed the alarm clock on his bedside table and listened as it tumbled to the floor, still ringing. He groaned and threw a pillow over his head. Sunday mornings were not meant for waking up early.

"Turn that thing off, would you?" Martha growled before slamming a pillow onto her head as well.

"It was your idea to get up this early." George leaned off of the side of the bed and silenced the irritating noise. He pulled the covers off of his body and stood, feeling the warm sun on his back.

"For heaven's sake, George, put some clothes on." Martha turned to look at George who was standing in merely his plaid boxers.

"Why Sunday, Martha? Of all the days you could have chosen to do this, why Sunday?" George rubbed his groggy eyes trying hopelessly to make the tiredness go away.

"I already explained this to you yesterday." Martha pulled the covers off of her body and stumbled to the bathroom.

"You haven't seen the guy since you were fifteen, Martha! What does he matter to you now?" George yelled through the house as he fished through his drawers for a pair of pants.

Martha opened the bathroom door and poked her head out, "I hold grudges, George. No one is going to make me look like a fool and forget about it. Even *after* they're dead."

George huffed exasperatingly and zipped up his trousers. Martha was nothing like George when it came to certain aspects. George could forgive someone in the blink of an eye while Martha could take her entire life and still remember every little mistake you've made. It wasn't normal, how Martha kept grudges like her life depended on it.

One time, about nine years ago, George had made the mistake of telling Martha that he had cheated on a woman he had been with for two weeks.

"You should feel ashamed," She had said, "that girl was probably hoping you'd propose to her someday." She didn't talk to him for a week after that, and she still brought it up occasionally, so he knew he wasn't forgiven.

"Are you ready to go yet?" Martha called from the bathroom and shuffled slowly into the hallway.

"As ready as I'll ever be. What are you wearing?" George's question was answered as Martha walked into the bedroom, dressed in a long black gown.

Martha's raven black dress was flowy and elegant. A delicate lace trim matched perfectly with her jet-black stiletto heels and sheer veil that rested on her head.

Martha waved her hands around her dress accentuating its beauty, "Just one finishing touch," she whispered and placed a beautiful diamond necklace upon her neck, "Ta Da!" She rested her hands on her hips and sauntered over to George, "Look familiar?"

"David's mother's necklace. You are an absolute psychopath, Martha."

"Possibly, but at least I'm a psychopath with good taste." Martha walked out of the room and towards the front door, "I'm leaving with or without you!"

George scurried hurriedly to her side and locked the door behind him.

• • •

"I still don't understand why, out of all of the boyfriends you had in high school, this *Henry* is such a big deal." George's stare was harsh as he looked at the road in front of him.

"Henry was my first love, George. He was the first boy who I truly believed I was in love with. Sure, it very well could have been puppy love, but it meant something to me. To me he was my top priority. He was also the first boy I had ever allowed to meet my father, which was a big deal considering how embarrassed I was of my home life." Martha looked down and fiddled her thumbs.

"I understand he was a big deal to you Martha, but it's been seventeen years. I'm sure there are a few people you've dated who have passed away or are in bad condition." George's voice was monotone, no compassion or grief apparent.

"Well, George, Henry was different from the others, and not only because he met my parents. Henry cheated on me with a freshman girl." Martha's stare was long and hard when she looked at George. "At the time, I was devastated. I had become the laughingstock of the school. Everyone knew that Martha Clark, the sophomore, had been cheated on with a freshman. Her name was Phyllis Miller. Phyllis was one of the girls who wore bright pink lipstick and smacked her gum like her life depended on it. She was the cheer captain and almost every football player wanted her. Her mother was a floozy and excuse me for saying so but I wouldn't be surprised if it rubbed off on her."

"With all due respect, Martha, kids do that all the time. Besides, we're in Kansas. You've never even been to Kansas until now so why is he buried here?" George threw up his hand in confusion.

"He married Phyllis fresh out of high school and moved here once it was official. When he passed away, I wasn't even invited to his funeral." Martha's voice was bland and cold.

George let out a rush of air, "Welp. We're here."

Martha opened her door and stepped onto the damp soil. Hundreds of gravestones lined the black metal fence. The breeze was cool and the smell of fog settling on the grass whirled in the air. The trees were dying, their leaves depressed by the fall weather.

"Start looking, George. Last name is Wilson." Martha began to stride in between the headstones, looking for the one that belonged to her past lover.

"Is this it?" George hollered from halfway across the graveyard.

Martha hurriedly jogged to his side and examined the name on the grave, *Henry Wilson.*

"Sure is," Martha snickered as she turned her head slightly to the right and saw the grave next to his. "and look who's right by his side." *Phyllis Wilson.*

"They have the same date of death." George whispered, afraid to break the calm silence the graveyard withheld. "How is that possible?"

"House fire." Martha said casually, the silence didn't mean as much to her. "The police say it was a candle that had been left burning for far too long."

"Tragic." George's whispers faded into the wind as he spoke.

"It wasn't a candle." Martha said bluntly, "It was the kitchen stove. Henry hates candles."

George watched as Martha's hands tightened into a fist and she pursed her lips. His eyebrows furrowed and he could tell that somewhere inside of her an emotion other than hatred had allowed itself to come up to the surface, hurt.

"Martha, I think it's time to leave." George placed a gentle hand on her back in an effort of comfort.

"You go back to the car. I'll be there in a moment, I want to say my goodbyes." She turned to look at George with sorrowful eyes.

"Very well then." George trekked through the mud back to the car.

Once Martha heard the car door slam, she pulled a pack of cigarettes out of her pocket. Along with the cigarette box came a small silver lighter, just big enough to fit perfectly in her palm. She lit her cigarette and stood for a moment looking at the two graves.

"You really did it Henry. You found the love of your life and kept to your vows. Until *death* do us part." Martha tapped the glowing red ashes of her cigarette onto the ground. "I wonder sometimes, Henry, what would have happened if you didn't make that mistake all those years ago." Martha raised the cigarette to her mouth, but then lowered it again and began to speak, "Maybe I would have turned out different. Maybe I would have never met James and all of this chaos could have been spared. Lives could have been spared. But you made the mistake. And here we are now. Now you're nothing but an old sack of dust and bones." Martha tossed her cigarette onto Henry's grave and turned towards the car, ready to forget him forever.

• • •

The next morning Martha woke up to find George hadn't gone to work that day. She walked into the living room and found him sleeping on the couch.

"George? Don't you need to be at work?" Martha nudged George's shoulder trying to wake him up.

George's eyes fluttered open slowly and he stared back up at Martha, "I threw up three times last night. I already called in sick."

Martha's brows furrowed and she held her hand to George's forehead. "You are a bit warm. Maybe a day to rest will be best." After flipping on the television Martha scooted George's legs over and sat down on the crushed blue velvet sofa.

George watched as the color drained from Martha's face. "Well, you look like you've seen a ghost." George chuckled.

Martha simply pointed at the TV and they both began to listen to the woman on the television.

"The Abilene Community Cemetery was found in flames yesterday at one fourteen P.M. The fire was finally put to a stop at two thirty P.M. Police say they have no lead on whether or not the fire was accidental. It is believed that the flames spread quickly due to the recent drought and leaves that had fallen. First responder, William Alden, states, "Let the deceased have their peace." If you have any information on the fire or who may have caused it, please report it to the Abilene Community Police Department. We'll be back."

The TV switched to a commercial break and George stared at Martha with pure hatred in his eyes. He stood and kicked the coffee table onto its side with a loud crash. His hands went to his hair and he paced the room shaking his head.

"Do you ever quit?!" George yelled so loud he thought he heard a glass breaking. George walked over to Martha on the couch and stood directly in front of her. He pointed at her; his finger so close to her that he could feel her breath. "You *have to* stop." He whispered angrily.

Martha stood, forcing George to take a step back, "I never meant for that to happen, George." She walked into the kitchen and opened the refrigerator, pulling out a glass bottle of milk.

George walked into the kitchen and gripped the counter, "How do you expect me to believe that?"

When Martha looked into George's eyes she could see he had been completely engulfed in hatred and anger. "I lit a cigarette and threw it on the ground before I walked back to the car. It must have caught fire on a leaf." Her voice was calm and matter of fact.

George turned and stomped out of the kitchen. "What are you doing?" Martha questioned, following him into the living room.

"Going to work." George muttered.

"But you're sick." Martha laid a hand on George's arm in a sense of comfort, but she was shoved off just as quickly.

George spun to look at her, their faces so close he could see every last detail of her right down to the texture on her skin. "I would rather go to work deathly ill than to sit in a house with a complete psychopath."

And just like that Martha was left to contemplate those words until her brain wouldn't process them any longer.

Craig

"If life has taught me anything, it is that you do not speak on experiences you never had the chance to experience."

June 25, 1957

The thick strip of sunscreen settled upon the bridge of Martha's nose slid ever so slightly as the sun beat down on it. Though eighty-three degrees **was** the average for late June in Kansas, George would never get used to it.

"I'm going to the supermarket to buy some more ice; do you need anything?" George hollered from across the front yard.

"How about some bleach, gloves, and trash bags?" Martha sneered and looked at George through the brim of her sunglasses.

"That's not a funny joke Martha. What could you possibly need that for?" George shifted his weight to his right foot and propped his hand on top of his hip.

"For cleaning, George! What else might I need it for?" Martha now stood from her yellow and orange striped lawn chair and mimicked George's body language, throwing her opposite hand into the air for exaggeration.

"Fine," George huffed, "I'll buy you the stuff. But so help me God, Martha-"

"Nothing out of the ordinary, George. I promise."

"That's exactly what I'm afraid of." George settled into the driver's seat of his car and slammed the door before heading off towards the store.

Martha's bare feet picked up damp pieces of grass as she walked across the yard to turn the sprinklers off. Her cardinal red nails shone brightly in the sun as she removed the lipstick smudged cigarette from her lips.

"That's some garden you got goin' there." A delicate voice called from behind her. A scrawny, blonde, shaggy haired man stood motionless at Martha's white picket fence. "Did you grow it yourself?" He asked once more.

"Did anyone ever tell you it is awfully rude to sneak up on someone?" Martha sauntered towards the man with a blissful look in her eye.

"Well, I'm sorry miss I didn't intend to startle you." The man spoke frantically, stumbling over his own tongue.

"Calm down, I was simply teasing you. Anywho, yes, I did grow it myself. Are you interested in gardening?" Martha leaned against the fence and trailed her cigarette back up to her lips.

"I find it quite interesting, yes. I have one of my own actually." The man said proudly.

"A young man like you has a garden? Shouldn't you be more interested in rock n' roll music or taking a girl out for a coke? You look not a second over seventeen for heaven's sake." Martha snickered ever so slightly at the thought of a young teenage boy tending to his own garden for fun.

"Well, isn't that a compliment and a half?" The man guffawed, "I'm twenty-five years old, miss!" The smile plastered on the man's face was so large he could barely keep his eyes open.

Martha's eyes went wide, "You look very young for your age then! What did you say your name was again?"

"Craig Dickinson ma'am. And yours was?"

"Martha Clark." Martha's slender hand reached for Craig's, joining him directly above the fence for a handshake that was very abnormally long. "Please come in," Martha unlatched the fence's small metal lock and allowed the door to sway open. "Don't mind the mess over on the porch, I haven't had time to tidy up my belongings." Martha scurried fairly quickly to her small wooden box that she liked to call her garden.

"What mess? Your porch is tidier than most of the rooms in my home." Craig offered a comforting smile. "Wow." He exhaled deeply as he saw the box in front of him. "This is a wonderful set of plants you have here." Craig slowly crouched to his knees in front of the box and began inspecting each and every plant.

"You think so?" Martha questioned, "I'm a junky for plant species but I've never found anyone that has been interested in them quite like I am."

Mostly everything that came out of Martha Lynn Clark's mouth were nasty lies, but occasionally, she did decide to tell the truth. Ever since Martha had been a little girl, running away to the woods to find peace, she's always been intrigued by plants. Plants of any kind. Large, small, poisonous, harmless, colorful, bland, anything she could get her hands on. Once when she was young, her father found a lily flower that she had picked from the woods and kept in her room as a symbol of nature's beauty. This did not go very well as Martha's father was always drunk when he'd arrive home from a night of gambling.

"What is this?" He had spat. *"Did a boy from school give you this?"* And though she had protested it and insisted she found it on her own, he would not hear of it. *"I knew it, Martha. You're a worthless floozy just like your mother."* And that was that. He slammed the lily and its vase against the hard wall of her bedroom, and it was over with. That was the last time Martha had ever brought a plant into her home.

"I mean, these lilies are simply beautiful." Craig said, astonished at Martha's precise care for her garden. "Not even my garden could live up to yours." Craig stood and brushed the dust from his pants.

"I would love to see it sometime." Martha mentioned.

Craig's warm brown eyes bored into Martha as he thought about the recommendation. "I suppose that would be alright." Craig smiled lovingly at Martha.

"Brilliant." Martha waltzed towards the gate.

• • •

"This is it." Craig gestured towards his house. The walk from Martha's home to his had been very eerily quiet and consisted of many glimpses towards the sidewalk. "It's beautiful, Craig." Martha spoke with enthusiasm. "Is your garden in the back?"

"Yes. Just follow me and don't mind the untrimmed grass." Craig shoved his hands into the depths of his pockets and began his hike to the backyard. "Now I must warn you Martha my garden truly isn't much. Just because I have a great love for plants doesn't mean I can always scrape together the money to purchase them."

"I'm sure it will be lovely." Martha's smile couldn't seem to melt away. Craig had a charming impression on her, and she couldn't tell if it might have been because he was a younger man or because he shared a large interest with her, but whatever it may have been, she loved it.

"Well, this is it." Craig spread his arms out showcasing his much smaller wooden box.

Martha mocked his earlier movements and sank to her knees to inspect the plants. The greenery was planted in very proper rows and they were all labeled by small wooden popsicle sticks with their corresponding name. "Well aren't you Mr. Organized?" Martha said, astonished at the tidiness of his garden. "Oh and you have my favorite." Martha's hand grazed the soft pink petals of a lily that was strategically placed in the back corner of the small wooden box.

"Lilies? I must admit I saw you as more of a magnolia type girl, but I think lilies are extraordinary. That's why I've planted some." Craig dropped to his knees next to Martha and took a small pocket knife out of his pocket. With one swift motion he cut the lily's stem and handed the lily to Martha. "A beautiful flower for a beautiful lady."

As Craig handed Martha the flower and their hands collided, Martha felt as if a streak of lightning had been spread through her veins. An unnerving, but most amazing feeling sore through Martha's body making her feel as if she was lighter than a feather. Martha stared into Craig's eyes, searching for anything to tell her that he had felt it too.

Craig cleared his throat and looked back down at the box, "Are you thirsty? I have some lemonade inside." He grinned at Martha and began walking towards the house, leaving her to question whether what she had felt was truly real.

Nonetheless, she followed Craig into his home. As she walked through the entryway, she was stunned to see how beautiful everything was. Earlier he had explained his home as *"messy"*, but Martha could see any and everything besides a mess.

An ultramarine plush carpet lined the floor from wall to wall, a dark wood paneling raised to half the height of the walls and accented the carpet perfectly.

The other half of the walls were the color of just picked cotton and picture frames were strategically placed throughout the home.

"The kitchen is this way!" Craig called, snapping Martha's attention back to him immediately. Martha followed his voice through the home, admiring the bright pieces of artwork that hung on the walls as she passed them.

Once she walked into the kitchen, she was presently surprised to find that Craig was, in fact, human and that he did, in fact, have a few parts of his life out of order. A pan with leftover grease sat on his stove and a few plates and bowls sat in the sink, waiting to be washed. Martha's shoes clicked on the linoleum flooring, echoing throughout the small kitchen.

Craig opened the refrigerator and pulled out a tall glass pitcher of freshly squeezed lemonade. "Let me guess," Martha spoke, "you grew the lemons yourself?" She raised a brow and steadied her elbow on the counter behind her.

Craig tittered, "No, actually. A friend of mine grew them in his garden and had more lemons than he could handle." He swung a small cabinet door open to find an array of glasses perfectly arranged. Craig took one of the glasses from the cabinet and placed it on the counter before filling it with ice cold lemonade.

He handed the glass to Martha and watched as she took a long sip. Again. The stare that Martha had been talking about. The stare which made her feel like her heart was beating out of her chest and her palms began to sweat. There was no way that he wasn't feeling the same way. That his veins weren't flooding with the feeling of electricity and his heart wasn't begging to be set free from his shell of a body.

"Would you like to take a seat in the living room? It's more comfortable than standing around." A nervous chuckle exuded from his throat and he began walking out of the room. Once again, he had dismissed the feeling that engulfed Martha's entire being since the moment they met.

Martha followed Craig into the living room and let her feet touch the plush carpet once more. As they made it to the center of the room Craig turned around to face Martha. His face was so close to hers. Their lips were mere centimeters from each other, begging to unite in something as sweet as a kiss.

Martha's eyes met Craig's and she couldn't help but smile at the fact that he was staring back, directly into hers. After what seemed like decades, Craig's lips finally graced Martha's. The electric feeling that Martha had felt now punched her in the face, making her feel as if she was floating in space with nothing to worry her at all. That was until she opened her eyes.

Martha pulled away from Craig and focused her eyes on the picture behind him. Hanging on the wall was a photo of a beautiful young woman dressed in a long white lace dress. She was holding a bouquet of flowers in one hand and in the other, her husband's waist. Craig's waist.

The room began to spin and Martha could feel her cheeks begin to burn, a ringing pestered at her ears and she felt one thing. Rage. "Martha?" Craig questioned, "Are you okay?" He furrowed his brow and looked at Martha expectantly.

Though Martha's attention could not be obtained. She looked around the room, allowing her eyes to drift to the multiple pictures on the wall she had been too blind to see before. That's when she saw the one picture that made her chest heave with anger. A picture of a young girl, maybe five years old, standing between her mother and father on a warm summer day.

Within seconds Martha was transported to her childhood. She remembered the exact day that she overheard her mother on the phone with her grandmother. *"He's been seeing someone else,"* She had said, *"he came home last night, drunk as usual, and laid it all out for me. How long they've been seeing each other, all the lies he told me to go out with her, and worst of all, mother, he told me he planned to leave me with the children and get eloped."* The tears and strain in her mother's voice were enough to push Martha over the edge. At the mere age of twelve years old, Martha knew about the "other woman" her father had been seeing and she felt nothing but disgust and livid anger towards her.

"I am the other woman." Martha's voice was so quiet it could be carried away with the slightest breeze. Martha's

attention was now solely on Craig. "You have a wife!" Martha shouted, fury fuming from her breath. Martha shoved Craig's chest, making him topple back a few steps.

"Martha I can explain!" He pleaded, but Martha's decision had already been made.

"How could you do this?!" Martha seethed, "How could you do this to your daughter? You no good piece of trash!" Martha screamed, pushing Craig once more causing him to topple back onto a woven chair.

"Please, Martha, let me explain myself." Craig thrust his arms into the air in an attempt to calm her.

But Martha couldn't be calmed. She was in a state of fury, one that was powered by such deep personal roots it simply could not be dissolved. She ran to the kitchen, swinging open every drawer she saw to find a knife. She carefully lifted the blade from the drawer and held it tightly in her hand. Out of the corner of her eye, Martha could see the faint outline of Craig's body standing in the doorway.

"Martha," He said calmly, "think about what you're doing okay?" A nervousness seeped from his words that could not be disguised as anything but what it was.

Martha chuckled and looked at Craig, "Tell me, Craig, how calm do you believe your daughter would be if she saw you kissing someone other than her mother inside of her own home?" A hot, anger filled tear now streamed down Martha's pale cheek.

"Martha, I understand what you're saying but-" Craig had no time to speak. Martha inched towards him slowly, careful not to leave out any detail as she spoke.

"You don't understand, Craig. My father did this exact thing to my mother. It may hurt your wife." Martha shrugged. "It may hurt Your mother, your father, but I assure you, it will not hurt anyone as badly as it hurts that little girl."

Craig stood pressed against the floral scattered wall, his chest rising and falling rapidly as Martha got closer. "It will hurt that little girl's heart more than anyone's heart will have ever hurt before." Martha now pressed the tip of the knife to Craig's chest, applying just enough pressure to cause a small drip of blood to stain his shirt. Craig's face contorted in agony and he let out a belt of pure fear. "So now, Craig, I must make sure that your heart hurts ten times more than hers."

The shining silver blade slid deep into Craig's chest and he howled in pain before sliding to the floor and leaving a trail of his heart's ruby colored aching to paint the wall.

Just as Martha was about to pull the knife from his chest, loud sirens began shrieking outside. She jerked her head to the window to see red flashing lights and policemen stepping out of their cars. Her eyes grew with worry, and she sprinted for the back door, making her way hurriedly across the backyard and beginning her trip back home.

As she made her way down the sidewalk, she reached into her pocket to grab a cigarette hoping it would calm her nerves. She shoved her hands deep into her pockets and pulled out a cigarette, but something was missing. Instantly, she sank to her knees and began emptying her pockets on the grass. Everything was there. Everything except her lipstick.

\

Peter

"One step is all it takes."

July 1, 1957

"Could you explain to me again why we are moving?" It was easy to see that George was less than displeased with the move. It had been around a week since the incident with Craig occurred and Martha had been paranoid since.

"George I already told you, I'll explain once we get where we're going." Throughout the entire trip, Martha had been watching out the windows for anything that seemed abnormal. As she watched the bright green trees pass by her window, her eyes brightened when she saw the sign.

Welcome To Omaha Nebraska. "Finally." George huffed and slowed the car as he took in the scenery around him. "We're going to need groceries for tonight." George mumbled. "Will you run into the supermarket and get a few for us?" George pulled into the parking lot of a supermarket labeled *Piggly Wiggly* and brought the car to a halt.

"I think it would be better if you went in, George." Martha's eyes pleaded with the man sitting next to her. He would never let her down in a time of need.

"Martha, I drove you and I away from the one real chance we had at a normal life not even knowing why I must do so, and you can't even walk into a grocery store for me?" The frustration was dripping from George's voice.

"This will all make sense once I explain things." Martha sat a hand on George's arm gently.

"Explain them then!" George shouted and shoved Martha's hand from his arm. After all he had done for her, all he had risked and given up, the least he deserved was an explanation.

"I can't." Martha's voice was low and crackly, and it sounded as if she may have been on the verge of tears, but George could not bring himself to feel any type of sorrow for her.

He scoffed at Martha's pitiful stare and swung his door open, allowing his feet to graze the pavement. The car door slammed behind George so harshly that he thought he may have broken it, but he simply did not care. Nothing could disturb George more than the fact that Martha refused to give him the explanation he deserved.

George walked speedily to the store entrance, wanting everything but to be anywhere near that woman he had left in his car. As the large glass entrance came into view, George could see all of the advertisements plastered onto the store front. Papers speaking of lost dogs and wanted jobs, but there was one paper in particular that made the blood streaming through George's veins shiver. He looked around frantically, watching for anyone who may be paying attention. He then ripped the paper from the glass and bolted back to his car.

Once George's body touched the leather fabric of his seat he was panting rapidly.

Martha's eyes grew big and she looked at George worriedly, "Are you okay, George? You look frightened." Martha's eyes then drifted to the small piece of crumpled paper resting in George's hand.

"Oh, I'm not frightened Martha." George now turned the entirety of his body to face Martha and began to straighten the paper in his hands. "I am *livid.*" George now tossed the paper into Martha's lap.

Wanted For Murder:
Martha Lynn Clark
Dead or Alive

Martha let out an exasperated laugh, "I'm famous." A nefarious grin crept onto her face as she stared at the sign.

"I beg your pardon?" George did all he could not to laugh at the sheer foolishness that he was witnessing. "*You* are not famous, Martha. Marilyn Monroe is famous. Elvis Presley is famous. For God's sake, Martha, Frank Sinatra is still famous compared to you."

Martha tilted her head to the side and looked at George with her wicked stare. "*I* am going to be in history books someday, George. Children will learn of me for years to come. And when they do they'll see how much of a contribution I made to this world."

George had lost his patience. A contribution to the world? How could Martha allow her foolish brain to believe such a thing? "A contribution?" George hollered. "A contribution, Martha? Really? How in God's green earth do you think you have ever made a contribution?" George was speaking so furiously that small specks of spit had showered out of his mouth.

"I put people out of the misery of living in this world. I'm sure that they're having a much better time up above than they ever would down here." Martha now looked forward out of the windshield and crossed her arms defensively over her chest.

"How did the police even find you? You murdered Paul last year, don't you think they would have found out before now?" A puzzled look was stamped onto George's face.

Martha rubbed her neck nervously. The last thing she felt like admitting to George was that she had failed to "sober up" as he called it. Martha hated that he called it that. "Sobering up" wasn't for mass murderers and crime committers, it was for people with alcohol and drug addictions. People like Martha's father. People who no matter how much their family, or friends, or conscious told them to stop, their body simply said "no". Martha's body did not tell her "no". Martha's conscience didn't tell her that what she was doing was awful and unacceptable and that she needed to stop, it was like gasoline to her fire. Martha's conscience worked like quicksand. Whenever her family or friends told her to stop, to run, she sank deeper and fell further into her "addiction". There was no helping her.

"George, there's a reason we had to leave Kansas." Martha's voice trailed off as if she didn't want to speak of the topic.

"Martha, please don't tell me what I think you're about to." George's voice was strained, and his throat began to burn and close.

"I thought we had something George. He was different. He made me feel like no one ever has." Martha looked at George who now had tears forming at the brims of his eyes. "I wanted a normal life. I wanted to get better and put the past behind me, I thought he could give me that. Within the short time I knew him, I saw a future with him. With children running around and a house of our own, and I think he saw it too." Martha's eyes plead with George.

George reached for Martha's hand and held it in his, not bothering to hide his emotions any longer. The woman he loved, be it romantically or platonically had hurt him the absolute most. All he wanted was for her to live a normal life where she was happy and loved by whomever she chose to marry. "Then why, Martha? Why did you have to ruin it?" A pain filled tear rolled down George's cheek and splattered onto Martha's hand.

"*He* ruined it, George. He had a wife and he didn't even tell me. But worst of all, he had a daughter. I remember how it feels to have a father who respects your mother so little he goes after other women without even ending things with her first. After I left, I realized that I had dropped my lipstick by accident. I suppose they had my fingerprints in the books already due to my earlier shoplifting incident." Martha looked down, slightly ashamed. To Martha, life was simply a game. And in Martha's game, she was determined to have everything she needed to 'win'. Even if that meant testing the limits when it came to the rulebook and directions.

George silently acknowledged Martha with a nod and let her hand free. He turned back towards the steering wheel and wiped his eyes quickly before putting the car into drive and taking off towards their new secret life.

• • •

"Where do you think you're going?" Since the wanted sign went up, George had been extra careful to keep Martha out of everyone's sight.

"Out." Martha whispered and began opening the door to their small mobile home. Moving to Nebraska had turned out not to be such an amazing idea. George had found himself struggling to find a good paying job and after taking a part time spot at a local farm, the trailer park had become their new home.

"Yeah, that's funny. Close the door." George spoke from the small kitchen they obtained as he washed the food off of a plate from their dinner hours ago.

"It's late, George." Martha rolled her eyes and slammed the trailer door. "No one is going to be out."

"And that is exactly why you *won't* be going out." George smiled sarcastically and sat the plate in the drying rack.

"I'm a grown woman not a teenage girl. I can go out whenever I please, thank you." The smile plastered on Martha's face resembled the prior sarcasm George displayed.

"Oh right, because you wanted to be a grown woman when you decided to kill, oh let me see, how many men?" George now counted on his fingers and stared at the ceiling.

"That isn't funny, George." Martha glared a warning look into his direction and turned to open the door again.

"Martha I'm being serious; you can't go out." George stepped towards Martha and threw his hand into the air.

"I don't care if you're being serious. I haven't gone out in forever and I'm done with it." Martha now slammed the door behind her and began her walk out of the trailer park, leaving George to wallow in his worry.

The air outside was crisp and warm, leaving an intoxicating feeling on Martha's skin. Though alone time was something Martha found herself quite booked with, making the decision to be your own company was something she really enjoyed. Walking around town at night was something she also found herself doing more than usual. Of course, George had no idea this was going on behind his back. That is what truly made Martha feel like a teenage girl again. Having to sneak out behind George's back just to get some time to herself made her feel pitiful and everything but in control of her life.

The dim street light shone on Martha's face, enlightening her complexion as she stood on the sidewalk, closing her eyes and breathing in the fresh night air. For a split second, Martha could feel her soul rest and possibly even come to peace. But it was ripped from her grasp as quickly as it had come.

"Hey you!" A masculine, harsh voice called from beside her. In the alleyway she could see the silhouette of a large man running towards her. With little to no time to register what was happening, Martha's feet began to move, and she could feel herself running. Though, mentally she was still catching up with the situation.

Martha dared to look behind her and saw that the man was wearing a hat with a large black brim and a badge was pinned to his shirt. A policeman. "Stop this second in the name of the law!" He shouted, but Martha's ears refused to hear him. She continued running as fast as she could until she finally reached a dead end. The street had ended at a small shop and there was absolutely nowhere for her now to run.

Martha's hands dug into her small purse that hung on her side in search of her gun. Ever since the very first incident with James, George had begged

Martha to rid herself of the weapon and he even did so himself at one point, hiding it in places he was sure she would never look for it and telling her he had disposed of it. But even after the multiple times George had hidden the pistol, Martha never failed to find it once more.

Once she felt her fingertips brush against the cold black metal of the firearm, she wrapped her hand around the grip of the gun and pointed it directly at the police officer that was running after her.

"Stop where you are, and I won't have to pull the trigger." Martha's index finger rested on the trigger gently.

"Martha, you don't have to do this. This isn't who you are. You're Martha correct?" The officer crouched slightly and raised his hands in front of him as he slowly stepped closer to Martha.

"Yes, that's correct, and I said not to come any closer!" Martha was now shouting through the barrier her teeth had made.

"Listen, I understand that you are upset, okay? I really do, but taking my life isn't going to help yours."

"With all due respect, sir, you do *not* understand. You have absolutely zero idea about anything that my life has consisted of." Martha's voice was gradually breaking and becoming harder to interpret.

"Call me Paul, okay? I am here to help you. That's what policemen are for. And I do apologize for saying I understand you because you are completely right,

I have no idea anything you have been through. So why don't you let me hold that gun for you and we can talk it out together. Okay?" Paul now stepped slightly closer to Martha.

The sound of sheer petrification could be heard through the streets of Omaha as Martha Clark's finger nudged the trigger of her gun, causing Paul to topple over onto the sidewalk. Martha calmly trudged to Paul's side, watching as the man gasped for breath and held his chest, which now was furnished with a hole that could not be filled much like Martha herself.

Paul's bloodied hand reached out for Martha, begging his villain to now take the place of his hero. Martha glanced around her, taking in the crimson splattered sidewalk and the clothes draping over Paul's body that now drowned in his own blood.

Martha crouched down at Paul's side, lifting the hat that had fallen off his head onto the sidewalk and holding it in her hand. Martha placed the hat tenderly over Paul's face and held it there for multiple seconds as she waited for the little movement that his chest participated in to slowly fade away. She then stood, smoothing out her skirt and began walking hurriedly back to the trailer park.

Scott

"My mother told me never to say nasty things about others, no matter how much you may dislike them."

August 14, 1957

"Can you believe what they said about me?" Martha was shouting across the trailer at George who was simply trying to get ready for work.

"Yes, Martha, yes I can." The irritation that lingered around George's entire being was obvious.

"Why would someone ever say such awful things?" Martha now rested her back against the bedroom wall, reading the newspaper article as George continued getting dressed. "Last month was *treacherous* for the communities of Abilene, Kansas and Omaha, Nebraska."

George watched as Martha mocked the columnist of the newspaper, waving her hands in the air and sighing as she spoke. "Twenty-five-year-old Craig Dickinson was found dead in his Abilene home on June twenty-fifth with a single stab wound to his chest. The suspect, Martha Lynn Clark, was traced by a small ruby lipstick that had been dropped on the floor."

Martha's pitiful and victim worthy stare now turned to a mischievous grin. "See, George, I'm famous! This is the first step; my name is in the newspaper." Martha threw herself onto the bed and let out a blissful sigh.

"You do realize that this *fame* you speak of is not for the right reasons?" George had now finished clothing himself and was beginning to slide his boots onto his feet.

"Fame never comes for the right reasons, George. But it doesn't matter now. People know my name and they know what I have done, and whether my impact was good or bad or all of the above, I made an impact." Martha sat up and crossed her legs over each other, smiling at George joyfully. "Anywho, let me continue." Martha cleared her rigid throat, "The psychotic killer was then assumed to be the fate of Officer Peter Jones as he was found with a gunshot to his chest on Elmer Street in our very own town of Omaha Nebraska."

"I still refuse to believe that you shot a police officer." George mumbled. When George had found out what happened on that worrying night that Martha had up and left the trailer, he was fuming with anger.

"*I* refuse to believe that this man called me a *psychopath*." Martha began searching the page frantically, looking for the name of the man who wrote such an awful thing. "Scott Miller." Martha whispered deviously.

"Who?" George's attention was now entirely on Martha, soaking up every move she made and every word she said. How was he supposed to trust her with any name of any man given her track record of almost every man she's met before?

"Scott Miller," Martha said, "the writer of the newspaper article. He's the one who's a psychopath, don't ya' think?" Martha bolted her hands into the air angrily. "He's the one that's taking two innocent men's deaths and turning them into a publicity stunt or his own wealth. Think about the victim's families for goodness sake!" The newspaper shuddered as Martha shook it harshly in the air.

"You're telling him to think about their families?" Rage coursed through George's entire body. "What about you, Martha? Were you thinking about their families when you slaughtered them as if their life meant nothing to yours?"

Martha looked at George in astonishment, "George, I did their families a favor!" She slammed the newspaper down and stood from her spot on the bed, inching her face closer to George's face slowly.

"Just because your father let you down as a little girl and gave you a bad rap as to what the men in your life should be doesn't mean you get to punish any man who slips their way into your life." George's breath was humid as it brushed Martha's cheek.

Martha began to feel an unfamiliar sting in her eyes. She lifted her hand and gently touched her cheek, feeling a damp tear trail onto her fingertips. The last time Martha had remembered crying was when she was eight years old.

After a while of watching her mother taking beatings and blows from her father, she had decided it was enough. Martha tried to stand between them in hopes that the fighting would stop, but it didn't. Martha's father shoved her to the side, making her wrist twist and she had creamed out in pain. Martha cried over that moment more than any moment she ever had before. She cried for her painful wrist, she cried for her mother, but most of all she cried for her father. The man that she had watched in the eight years of her clipped childhood go from a magnificent, protective, father to a drunk, abusive, piece of trash. At least that was what she had made of him in her eight-year-old brain.

But now Martha was crying once more. And it wasn't for her father or her mother or all the men she had delivered a deceitful fate to. It was for herself. She cried for all of the awful experiences she had undergone and all of the treacherous scenes she had seen.

And now, though he may not have wanted to, George comforted Martha. He hugged her for the first time in years, rubbing her back soothingly and telling her that everything was going to be okay as long as they had each other.

"Martha, I understand that you couldn't help yourself when you were a child," George cooed, his chin resting upon Martha's shoulder. "But that's why you must help yourself now."

Martha's voice was muffled by the stiff fabric of George's shirt, "I can't, George." Martha's whole body shuddered against George's as if she was an orange fall leaf blowing in the wind, so close to falling off the branch.

George sighed in defeat. No matter what he did or how many extravagant stories he came up with of how wonderful Martha's life would be if she just let it fall into place would ever faze her. Martha was a statue. A stone statue that could never be moved or articulated by anything other than sheer force. But what would Martha's force be? George often sat awake at night just wondering what the final straw for Martha would be. So far, the only answers he had come up with were prison or worst of all, death.

"I best get going to work." George's voice cut Martha like a knife. Jolting her back into a sense of reality she found hard to swallow. She wouldn't cry for the next seventy years if it meant avoiding this type of embarrassment.

Martha detached herself from George's body, "Right."

George looked at Martha and widened his eyes when he saw the black river of makeup running down her cheeks. He carefully wiped it away with his thumb and began collecting his belongings for work.

•••

George opened the door to the trailer to find Martha standing in the living room, a paper pad and pencil in her hands. Around her were boxes full of miscellaneous items that had yet to be taped shut.

"No... no... no..." George's voice trailed off as he slammed his lunch box and thermos to the ground. The metal of the thermos made a large crashing sound that echoed throughout the entire camper. "What are you doing?" George yelled, frenzied.

"George, please have a seat and calm down." Martha perched herself upon the sofa's arm and patted the seat next to her with her hand.

"I am not calming down and I am not taking a seat. I *am* however going to know what is going on here right this very second." George's voice was deathly serious.

"We're moving." Martha thrusted her hands into the air before George had time to speak, "But, George, it's okay." Martha's voice was tactful as she spoke to George, careful not to upset him. "I already called someone, and they said that we could stay with them until we find a place of our own."

"It isn't a matter of where we live or what the expenses are, Martha." George pinched the bridge of his nose, convincing himself it did something to diffuse his anger. "It's a matter of *why*."

"Just like you told me earlier, I need to help myself. I think getting a fresh start somewhere that doesn't have disturbing memories tied to it would be best for my healing."

Anyone with an inkling of sense in their head would know better than to trust Martha Clark. Especially when she said she was going to change, since change is one of the things she had ultimately grown to hate.

"Who are we staying with? Oh, and more importantly what state are we moving to now?" George hated moving with a deep passion. Martha continuously dragging him around the states made him feel as if his life was a traveling circus act and he was the one clown that always had a frown upon its face.

"I called my sister." Martha was now burning holes into the floor with her stare. She couldn't bring herself to admit such a shameful act while looking into the eyes of her so-called best friend.

"Your sister?" George was puzzled. Though he had always known that Martha had siblings, she had never spoken to them. Ever since Martha brought it upon herself to leave the home of her dearest mother, she hadn't spoken to any of her family.

"Yes." Martha focused on the twiddling of her thumbs as if it was the most entertaining thing she had ever seen. "My little sister Eloise."

George was now in an even deeper state of confusion. There was a time when Martha would talk to George about her problems and one of the recurring ones was Eloise. Martha had always said that Eloise hated her since she left the home and Martha couldn't blame her either. She had left her little sister in a home with a melancholy mother and a drunk abusive father, how could she ever forgive her for that? Leaving her at a time she needed her most?

"She told me she had forgiven me for my young and naive mistakes, and she wanted to help me." Martha now stood from her position on the couch and exhaled a large breath. "Well now," she said with the most forceful grin she could muster, "you better get to packing." As Martha made her way down the small hallway and into the bedroom George followed behind her, grabbing her wrist and turning her around.

"Does she know?" George's voice was low and quiet as though even speaking of the matter in private could infiltrate everything in a matter of seconds.

Martha looked up at George through her eyelashes, a completely blank look on her face. "Know what?" Martha mockingly whispered, her bubblegum scented breath floating off her tongue.

"Martha, don't play stupid. You know exactly what I am talking about."

Martha wouldn't hear of the foolishness coming out of George's mouth. She raised her eyebrows inquisitively, waiting for him to voice his thoughts.

"The wanted posters, the newspaper articles, the fact that your one and only husband died suspiciously, and no one knows how that occurred. I mean come on Martha; she must have heard something by now!" George's voice broke the barrier of infiltration, no longer minding who heard their 'private' discussion.

"Whether or not she knows about my sudden rise to fame, I'm not sure. But I do know one thing. I have just broken her barrier of hatred and disgust and I refuse to let someone like you give her yet another reason to despise me again." Martha pulled her wrist from George's grip, allowing herself to walk back to the bedroom and begin packing once again.

• • •

George rubbed his groggy eyes and checked the clock. Twelve thirty-six in the morning. A loud crashing sound had awoken him from his much-needed sleep. "Martha?" George turned on his side, expecting to find Martha soundly asleep in bed, though he found the exact opposite.

Next to him on the bed was nothing but wrinkled sheets and a flattened pillow that was in desperate need of replacement. George was now wide awake, his brain running what seemed to be a million miles a minute.

"Martha!" George hollered, quickly attempting to wrap a robe around him and cover the indecency of his boxers. Another small clinking sound echoed in his ears and he began making his way out of the bedroom and into the small space they had to call a kitchen.

On the tile floor sat Martha, completely oblivious to the messy haired, robe covered man that stood in the doorway. In front of her rested a small, navy blue, canvas duffle bag which appeared to be nearly empty.

"Martha?" George's voice was soft once again as it had been when he lay in bed, barely awake.

Martha's eyes now lifted to meet him, and George saw something he hadn't seen before. He saw fear. He also saw a large, sharp, glistening kitchen butcher knife resting in her hand.

"Martha what are you doing?" George kneeled down in front of Martha's duffel bag and began rummaging through it.

"George, don't." Martha's hand touched George's shoulder pleadingly, but he wouldn't listen.

George began pulling items from the bag, his eyes growing angrier with each object that his hands came in contact with. Bleach, stain remover, rags, trash bags, gloves, knives, a gun, but most importantly the newspaper article that Martha had read earlier. He laid them all on the floor in front of him. "What are you thinking?" George whispered.

"This isn't fair, George. That Scott Miller freak gets to call me a psychopath for everyone to hear? I'll give them something to write about all right. *Columnist Scott Miller murdered after writing an offensive article on Martha the psychopath Clark.*" Martha raised her arms in the air as she said the dramatic title, acting as if she could envision it in her brain on a large theater screen.

"What happened to fixing things?" George was no longer mad, no longer hoping that Martha would change or even having hope that she someday could.

"I am going to fix things, George. But no one ever learns anything instantly. I'm going to need time and patience from everyone, especially you." Martha had a way of bending situations to her advantage. Her brain never missed a beat when it came to orchestrating the perfect lie in order to save her own behind.

George could no longer fight, no longer hold his emotions and instinctive feelings captive for ransom. So, there he was, hugging Martha and holding her as tight as he possibly could, in order to set those emotions and feelings free. "Just promise me that no matter what, you're gonna try." A single tear strayed from George's eyes, falling to his lips and making his emotions appear even more bitter tasting than they already were.

"I'm going to try George. *Promise.*"

Neil

October 29, 1957

Living in Eloise's house for the past two months had been complete and utter misery for George. Not only did Eloise and her husband, Frank, not approve of George and Martha's arrangement of living together before marriage, Eloise was five months pregnant and her emotions had more twists and turns than a roller coaster. Martha had explained to her many times that they were "just friends" and nothing romantic had ever occurred between them but they still refused to believe a word she said.

"I'm going out for a while, Martha. I'll be back before long." George grabbed his coat off the hook and allowed the fabric to hug his physic.

Martha was alone again, nothing to be surprised by. Frank was going to be at work all day and Eloise was at a doctor's appointment, checking up on the little baby inside her stomach.

Loneliness was something Martha had adapted to. Since she was a little girl, she had immersed herself in it. She allowed the space between her and everyone surrounding her to wrap around her like a security blanket that could never be pulled away.

"Be back before dinner." Martha called, knowing that George could care less about dinner and most likely would eat something while he was gone.

So, once again, Martha allowed the void that surrounded her to completely engulf her entire being. She allowed it to swallow her whole and use her to expand the void that could never be filled. Her eyes began to close, her eyelids slowly sliding downward until the entire room was no longer filled with chairs or couches or end tables and lamps, it was simply a black void that surrounded her, making her feel the most at home she'd ever felt before.

A loud knocking sound jolted her from her peaceful blanket of darkness, and she stood, opening the front door. Outside stood a man, maybe six feet tall, wearing a blue button up shirt that was cuffed at the sleeves and had stripes running up and down the collar.

The man's eyes looked up to meet Martha's and they widened when he opened the door. "You're Martha Clark." The man said breathlessly, his face whitening instantly as if he had seen a ghost.

"Martha who?" It was typical of Martha, to lie and cheat and scam people until her face turned blue.

"What are you doing in Frank's house?" The man now seemed panicked, distraught even thinking about what may have happened to the man he had once known to live here.

"Eloise is my sister; I'm staying with her for a while to help with the newborn when it arrives." Martha smiled charmingly, opening the door wider as she did so.

"May I ask who you might be?" Martha's gaze lingered on the man for a moment, searching his face for clues as to what he may be thinking.

"I'm Neil," he said hesitantly, reaching out his hand to greet Martha. "Frank and I are good pals. He said he was having a termite problem and I work at the local pesticide center." A small satchel was situated in his hand down at his side.

"Well isn't that nice? I was under the impression that Frank didn't have any *pals.*" A playful tone intertwined with her voice as she spoke, attempting to lighten the mood.

Neil chuckled, "Well I suppose I ought' to get going." He turned his back to leave.

"No," Martha butted in, grabbing his forearm to stop him. "Please come in. Frank won't be home for a while and thinking about all of those little pests running around makes my skin crawl."

Neil turned around, looking at her inquisitively. It was almost like he couldn't decide if he wanted to love or hate her, but his brain must have chosen love because he allowed himself to slip past Martha and into the living room.

Martha carefully shut the door behind him, locking the small golden knob as she did so. This went completely unrecognized by Neil, who was now sitting on the small powder blue loveseat facing the television and the sheer curtains that hid him from the outside.

"Let me take that for you." Martha offered sweetly, gently grabbing the handle to Neil's bag resting in his hand, but Neil's fingers didn't budge their grip.

"With all due respect, ma'am, the chemicals used for extermination are extremely toxic and can only be handled by professionals." His eyes seared holes into Martha, judging her silently. "Which you are not."

Martha's eyes narrowed like they never had before, she already didn't like this *pal* of Frank's. "Well then," Martha huffed, letting go of her grip on the bag and straightening her posture. "Would you care for something to drink? Milk perhaps?" Martha tilted her head eerily.

The tension between Martha and Neil had grown astronomically in the small amount of time they had known each other. Here she was, letting this man whom she'd only known for mere minutes make her look like a fool.

"Milk would be fine, thank you." Neil's eyes watched and studied Martha carefully as she walked away, fading into the kitchen. Something about her had seemed off to him. She looked so oddly similar to the woman in the news that he found it hard to believe that she could have been anyone else.

Neil's juniper green eyes searched the room curiously, hoping to find something that could put his agitated body at ease. His sight trailed to the coffee table sitting in front of him and he froze, wondering if what he'd laid his eyes upon were real.

On the front page of the weekly newspaper was an image of a young happy looking woman with a vexatious grin spread widely across her face. This was the woman that was killing innocent men around the country just for her own entertainment. This was the woman that was standing ten feet away from Neil, preparing him a glass of milk in his *pal's* kitchen. Neil watched patiently as this same exact woman walked through the living room entryway and sat a tall glass of milk in front of him on the coffee table.

"Drink up," she said, "milk isn't very tasty once it's warm." The smile on her face displayed kindness. It displayed softness and warm heartedness and everything that could fit between. But the smile on her face was not kind or soft or warm hearted in the slightest. The smile on her face was the same smile that had appeared when all the other men that had fallen into her trap saw before they took their very last breath. Just like Neil would do if he didn't get out.

"Wouldn't you look at the time? I must be getting back to work, they'll wonder what's happened to me." Neil looked at his watch briefly, barely giving himself enough time to read the hands his clock displayed.

Martha's eyes shot spears into Neil, the tension growing like never before. "Won't you at least drink some of your milk?" Martha was still positioned neatly in front of the coffee table, scooting closer at the mention of him leaving without drinking his beverage first.

"I've seemed to have lost my thirst." Neil cleared his throat and stood slowly, inspecting every movement Martha made as if a single flick of her wrist could be the next worldly depression.

"Isn't that a shame." Martha leaned closer to Neil, grabbing the glass of milk and beginning to walk back into the kitchen.

"I'll let myself out." Neil commented after her, relieved to be in the room alone once again.

"I could never be such a bad hostess." Martha commented back from her spot in the kitchen. Careful to not make a sound, Martha slowly opened the silverware drawer and slid her fingers around the rough handle of a knife. "Please let me walk you out." Martha's arm snaked around her back holding the knife upside down just like she had so many times before.

Neil watched as the figure of the woman walked back into the living room. He was now standing next to the couch merely steps away from the front door. From freedom.

Martha inched closer, the malicious grin upon her face growing with every step. Neil's eyes took in her figure, noticing the arm that was now stretched behind her back.

Just then, being polite did not matter to Neil. Nothing mattered to Neil other than getting out of Martha's house and back to his own safety. Neil's hands pooled with sweat, his ears beginning to feel as if the sun was beating upon them.

"Are you okay Neil? You look like you've seen a ghost." A glimmer of light reflected from the blade that Martha now exposed to the man standing in front of her. The look in her eyes resembled that of a lion's whose prey stood directly in front of them, trembling as they prepared to take their very last breath.

Neil didn't care to respond. How could he? Here he was, standing in front of a woman who had been deemed 'deathly' and praying that he would be the one man to survive her wrath.

Neil's hand reached for the small golden knob placed on the door, slipping as he attempted to turn it. He looked back at Martha, panicked to see that she had gotten closer during his struggle to open the door. Neil's fingers fiddled with the doorknob, desperately trying to turn the handle and let himself free.

A hand grazed Neil's shoulder. *No.* The only word soaring through Neil's mind when he felt Martha's sharp deathly nails dig into his collar bone.

"Going somewhere?" Martha's words entered Neil's ears and invaded his brain, making him feel as if he was standing at the edge of a cliff and could be launched over the side at any time.

"Yes." Neil whispered, squeezing every ounce of courage from his body as he did so.

"I beg your pardon?" Martha's grip on Neil loosened slightly, obviously surprised to hear his response.

Neil said nothing more. He turned quickly and shoved Martha, sending her reeling onto the floor. His ears winced as he heard Martha's painful shriek. But he couldn't turn and look at her. He couldn't wait a single second more and risk his life as well as many others.

Quickly, Neil unlocked the door and turned the knob, smiling slightly as he felt a gust of wind on his cheek.

• • •

The door remained agape in front of Martha, making her shiver as the cold October breeze flowed into the room and over her body. She looked down at the blood trailing from her thigh. Her hand quivered as she attempted to pull the knife from her wound, but she screamed in pain. It was useless. Martha's eyes wandered to the blood-stained carpet below her. The familiarity of this situation struck her all at once. A blood-stained carpet, a sharp kitchen knife piercing through the flesh of another human being. Yet this time that human being was not dead. That human being was alive and breathing and fully aware of what had occurred and most of all that human being was Martha. Not James or David or Robert or Paul or Craig or Peter. *Martha.*

George

"Goodbye."

October 29, 1957

"Martha?" George's tall lanky figure stood in the entryway of the living room. "Oh my God." He kneeled next to Martha, taking her hand in his. "What happened?" Tears began to well in his eyes.

Martha was surprised. She expected anger and fury to be thrown at her, but she got the exact opposite. "Don't worry about it." Martha shook her head, attempting to sit up on her elbows.

"Don't worry about it?" George looked bewildered. "What in God's name do you mean *don't worry about it?*" The wild look in Martha's eyes as she lay there on the floor was slowly getting to George.

"Listen, George, I need you to close the door and lock it. Close all of the windows, draw the curtains, everything."

George panicked. As he went around the room obeying Martha's orders his mind was frantic thinking of every possibility. Did someone find out Martha's whereabouts and come here searching for revenge? But if so, who? A family member of the deceased? George could wrap his brain around it.

"Okay George now I need you to get me off this putrid floor and somewhere safe. We need to leave. Now." Martha's voice was stern and demanding not wasting a single second to give orders.

"Martha, please calm down." George could no longer contain his questions.

Martha shook her head, her frail body still losing blood. "Please George just take me somewhere safe and I will explain everything."

George looked at the woman pleadingly. How could he wait? Of all the deranged things that Martha had done over the years he'd known her, this was the final turning point. He could no longer sit around waiting for explanations just to be let down when she promised they wouldn't happen again.

"No Martha." George was used to feeling small as he stood by Martha's side. But now, he felt as if he was tall enough to reach the clouds. "I want to know what is going on and I want to know now."

Pure trepidation was coursing through Martha's body. Why couldn't he just listen? He always listened. "You wanna know what happened George? Here's what happened. One of Frank's friends, Neil, came over to see Frank. I told Neil that Frank wasn't here and he asked me if I was the horrid serial killer woman that everyone had been talking about in the news." Martha's voice quivered with agony as she glanced down at the knife lodged into her leg. "I told him no and he came inside for a moment after I offered him a drink."

George's eyes were concentrated on Martha like they never had before. "And then?" George questioned, anxious to know every last detail.

"It was supposed to happen like normal, George, I swear!" Hot tears began rolling down Martha's face, glossing over her eyes and eyelashes.

"Martha," George's voice was deathly low as he questioned her, dreading the answer he may receive. "Where is Neil?"

Martha looked George directly in his eyes, hoping to get through to him the urgency of her voice. "He's gone, George. He left. He's most likely at the police station this very second telling them exactly where to find me!" Martha could no longer stop the tears from stinging her eyes, no longer ignore how familiar they truly were.

George looked Martha in her eyes, panicked. Reflections of a red flashing light shone in Martha's water falling eyes. It was as if Martha's voice had beckoned them herself. "We have to go." George said pressingly.

Martha bit her lip in an attempt to silence her pain as George picked her up from the floor and began carrying her through the hallway. A loud pounding could be heard from the living room, or was that George's heart? He couldn't tell.

George had waited for this moment for years. The moment that Martha Clark would slip up, leave something behind, give someone reasoning to question her charming facade. And though he'd waited for this day, dreamt of it over a million times and imagined it just as much, his moment of bliss and clarity was everything but. It was sorrowful and cloudy and made his vision blurry with concern.

George reached one of his hands carefully to open a small door, leading downwards to a basement. He rushed, walking as fast as he could without dropping Martha to the end of the stairs.

George's feet relaxed upon the cold pavement. The basement was dark and gloomy, dependent on one small lightbulb to radiate the entire room. The walls were made of a thick and cold gray cement that echoed when you so much as whispered a word.

George pulled a small wooden crate from the corner, resting Martha onto it carefully. "Try to calm yourself." George turned, running up the small flight of cement stairs and locking the door.

When George returned to the bottom of the stairwell, he saw Martha sitting there in agony, her leg extended in front of her. "This is going to hurt." George whispered, slipping his shirt off his back and ripping it into two. "But this is the best option."

Martha gripped the sides of the crate, bracing herself for what she was about to endure. George's hand slipped around the knife situated in Martha's thigh, releasing a shaky breath before sliding the blade out from her leg, his heartbeat muffling her screams.

"Oh my God." Martha mumbled, relieved to have the blade freed from her body.

George quickly wrapped his jaggedly ripped shirt around Martha's leg, tying it as tightly as he could to stop the blood flow. He looked at the blade in his hand, dripping with blood of someone so dear to him. He laid it carefully upon a storage shelf just behind him. He crouched down beside her, "Martha," George whispered, looking her dead in the eyes. "I think we both know how this will end." His voice was thick and shaky, the words barely squeezing their way from his throat.

"George, please." Martha placed a hand on George's shoulder, forcing herself to look down at the cold hard ground.

"If we never speak again, I need you to know this." George's hand rested on Martha's knee, gliding his thumb over it soothingly.

Crashing could be heard overhead, along with the mumbling of faint voices and footsteps trailing around the house.

"Help me to my feet." Martha uttered, attempting to push off of George's shoulder.

"Martha, no. You're in absolutely no condition to stand." The worry was pooling around George's voice.

"George," Martha said warningly. "Like you just said, we may never speak again. If it is my dying wish to stand then I will stand." Her voice didn't alter as she commanded George sternly.

George didn't care to argue. He lifted Martha to her feet, holding her up by her waist.

"As you were saying," Martha peered into George's eyes, taking in every word he muttered.

"As I was saying," George took a deep breath, challenging himself to finally announce what he'd wanted to for years. "Martha, all I ever wanted was a chance. A chance to be the man that you had searched for. You've spent the past seven years of your life looking for love and all I wanted was for you to notice that it was here the whole time." George's eyes welled with tears; his emotions displayed on his face as was his pain from the years he'd spent silent.

Martha watched him closely, allowing the words that he spoke to touch her in a way she'd never been before. She allowed them to touch her heart.

"Martha, all I've ever wanted was for you to be happy. So, I watched you with those men, destroying the lives of so many people, mine included. But worst of all, I watched you destroy yourself. I watched you transform from the girl I had known and loved to some hideous beast who had no compassion or sympathy."

Martha winced at those words. She hated that he referred to her in that way, speaking of her as if she was some type of animal.

"And though you took everything from me, my entire life down the drain before the age of fifty," George paused, he'd never felt this way before. As if he was drowning in his emotions and the only way to get back to the surface, to breathe, was to let the words fall from his mouth, "I love you."

Martha hugged George tightly, embracing him in a way she'd always wished someone had with her. Through her years of childhood, when she felt unloved and useless. Through her years with James, when she swore her father was right and she was nothing more than her mother had been. And through her years with George, when she felt the most loved she ever had, but she was loved at a distance. Loved from a distance so great, her heart couldn't return the favor.

As George's head lay on Martha's shoulder, tears leaving small speckled water spots upon her blouse, Martha reached her hand out towards the silver metal storage shelf in front of her.

"Martha?" George questioned, feeling the absence of her hand on his back. George lifted his head, looking Martha dead in the eyes.

Martha grinned at George warmly before plunging the glistening blood-stained blade into his back.

A concerned, hurt look crossed George's face just before he fell to the floor. Martha held onto the storage shelf ensuring that her balance could not be altered.

Throughout Martha's life she had been disappointed by people, taken advantage of, pushed around, and had her trust broken by many. Though, once she had grown, she found that not all people would break her trust. Not everyone would treat her heart like it was a metaphor to be tossed around and used whenever they may please. George was one of those people. He cared for Martha's heart, took care of it possibly more than she did herself. But when you're brought up in a world where a stranger is more like a friend and family is nothing but blood, love is nothing but a word.

Martha's arm reached out for the long string hanging from the light bulb. She rested her hand around it, looking down at George with a loving smile. "Goodbye, George."